Tinker Tales

Tinker Tales

OF MOTORCYCLES AND MAGIC

Allan Lowson

To order additional copies of this book, contact:
Xlibris Corporation
1-888-795-4274
www.Xlibris.com
Orders@Xlibris.com
46926

Contents

Dedication

To the memory of Albert Emett, who mentored a young biker, and Jim Fogg, who encouraged the writer.

DIE SCHWARZWITWE

Sun in the face, moolah in the pockets, and a factory-fresh one lung pony between the legs—what more could a road-gypsy want? Royal Enfields Bullets weren't the fastest iron even when they still made them in Redditch; 'Rolling Oilfields' the old wet-sumpers were called. The parent factory failed in 1970 and the Madras branch in India hadn't spiced them up any. Tinker had picked this one up new on a deal, however he preferred original bikes and could use a more potent ride. That was his business: classic bikes, parts, literature and memorabilia appraised, bought, and traded.

He pulled into the parking lot with a thirst. The 'Nelson Touch' was a free house and, as the shingle suggested, turned a blind eye to the eccentricities of its clientele. Even hairy, be-leathered bikers were welcome, providing they didn't try warming their hands on the barmaid's tits. Tinker shook out long, coal-black curls and combed fingers through his beard for bugs. A smile lit a swarthy face as he espied the pump handles. This week's guest beer turned out to be Taddy Porter, a black charmer from the brew-kettles of Tadcaster.

A flash of colour caught his eye as he bellied up to the bar. Red the Ted, of course, over by the window and waving his empty glass. Tinker added another pint and a couple of packets of pork rinds to his order, then carried them over to the table. Red had left a message about a strange bike for sale. Old, big, black and weird—Tinker's kinda bike.

Edward 'Red' Diamond had the build and colour sense of a Rubik cube. However it wasn't been the scarlet drape jacket that earned him the moniker, it had been his hair. Not that you'd guess now, the silver jelly roll and immaculately coiffured duck's arse suggested more powdered Regency than macassared Edwardian. The last time they had been scarlet was in the application of involuntary rhinoplasty to an unfortunate opponent. Red had always been the bar fighter *par excellence*. Pork sausage fingers curled around the pint and faded H.A.T.E. tattoos from his Borstal boy days stood out. A man better to call friend than enemy. He'd be in the pub every Saturday afternoon while Shirl got on the steak and two veg.

"So, Red," Tinker ventured, "where is this mate of yours with the Vinnie?" Red had never been a Rocker; big Yank V-8s were more his style. Still, how many bikes are just a polished black engine with a wheel at each end? From his description it had to be a Vincent, and a 'special' at that. Tinker could feel a tingling in his bones: it sounded wicked.

"Chuck'll be along, my old son, even if he's a bit slow," Red chuckled. "I told you to come early so you could get 'em in." He held up a freshly emptied glass—finder's fee.

He'd swilled another two out of Tinker by the time a well-crunched Ford transit van smoked into the lot. Chuck turned out to be a barrow boy hustling a few quid any way he could.

"So anyhow," Chuck gurgled around a slurp of ale. It seemed Tinker would be buying for everyone today. "I see this bloke in torn leathers, see. Looks like he got thrown down the road sumfin' chronic, and he's just hopping mad." Another slurp. "I reckon he's hurt 'is head, concush . . . , like what happened to me, 'cos he's raving away. Can't understand much, Jerry bloke, see. Shaking and swearing terrible, he is. Stuff like '*Schwarz teufel*' and '*gottverdamnt Englische rad*'. See, I can remember new stuff pretty good. Well, I saw a chance for a deal."

Chuck looked at them for approval. "I gorra make the extra dosh what with the kid coming an' all. Funny thing is though, I don't have to dicker or nuffin'. He doesn't want the bike, won't even go near it. I can't remember much about bikes since the accident, but even all banged up, I just wanted it. I could tell it were real special, like." Chuck beamed at his acumen. "Jerry pulled out the papers right there and then, said he'd sign anything, in blood if he had to. I got it for five hundred quid, even I knew it were worth more—only it was my mate Magic John's money I'd been holding for him. So I gorra move it before he finds out." He glanced at Tinker uncertainly; a big, gypsy-looking biker does little to inspire confidence. "Red says you wouldn't screw me."

Tinker looked at Red, and nodded. Frankly Chuck didn't put a rise in the Levis.

So, out to the van and Chuck opened the back. Tinker didn't know this Magic John character, but his investment seemed safe. Whoa boy! A series 'B' Vincent Black Shadow. World's first road going motorcycle designed exclusively for suicidal nutters, plus it didn't seem damaged at all. Mind you, it wasn't exactly stock, kinda gothic café racer that oozed viciousness like pitch.

Tinker got in and checked some more. No sign of road rash, no bent controls, 'no nuffin', as Chuck would say. Chuck pulled out the papers—curiouser and curiouser! It had just come from Argentina and seemed to have got through plenty owners. Certainly no-one seemed to have kept it long.

Grabbing the bike, Tinker jerked back as if shocked from a plug wire and nearly had it over. He cursed Chuck's acrylic shag carpeting and useless anti-static chain—a few links short like its owner.

"Watch out for the side stand, it's not steady," warned Chuck. "Bleedin' fing lunged forward coming over, nearly put me into a pole. I thought I was a goner, I did." Having seen his version of a secured load, Tinker wasn't much surprised, Chuckie wouldn't be making Queen's Scout with those knots.

However, fortune favours fools. After hauling out the bike, Tinker walked around it with growing awe. Everything polished black as sin except for a curious emblem, the colour of Red's drape, on the leather tank cover. Could be an hour glass or a dice shaker, bit like that poisonous spider marking. One thing for sure, this terrible panther had clearly been evolved for one purpose alone—brute speed.

Tinker's jaw kept dropping. Someone had fitted fuel injection and triple discs, yet there seemed something wrong with the engine. Counting the fins, he realised the barrels had been dropped about an inch. "Bugger me blind," he exclaimed. "It's a short rod."

"Izzat like hot rod?" Chuck wanted to know. Not too far off the mark; they run hotter but rev higher and go faster. Tinker's fingers still tingled, but he didn't care. Man-eater or no, he had to twist this pussy's tail to hear her howl. A little burn-up before purchase, yes? He could start any bike, he could.

Those weren't his thoughts a second later, writhing on the ground and clutching his knee while the backfire still rang in his ears. Then there was the laughter. He must have looked pretty funny, but did it have to sound so diabolic?

Red lifted him up, and the twitch in his face wasn't from the effort. "You're the hard man, Tink," he said approvingly. "I don't think many would be able to laugh that off."

Tinker took his weight, and the pain made him snap at Red. "Yeah, right. Don't try to kid me. It was you, howling like a tart."

Anger suffused the big ted's face, highlighting white battle scars. The pain in Tinker's knee suddenly seemed less important.

"It must have been Chuck," Red growled. "And the last bloke as called me a nancy-boy is still eating through a straw."

Tinker felt quite willing to blame Chuck, only he didn't seem amused, in fact he looked the picture of misery.

"I got nuffin' to larf about," he moaned. "It's a jinx bike like that Jerry tried to tell me. You won't want it now and I'll be lumbered with it. John said he'd turn me into sumfing 'orrid if I blew his dosh."

"Then it's not your lucky day, sunshine," said Red, waving at a lanky blond bloke about to enter the pub. "Over here, Johnny boy."

Chuck groaned aloud. Tinker felt less impressed with the guy's Bogart act: dirty flasher's mac, tie at half mast, fag dangling out the corner of his unshaven mouth. Then he came close enough to look in the eyes. Crazy eyes—this bloke would be capable of anything.

"'lo Chuck," John drawled. "Where's my loot then?"

Red and Tinker turned to look at Chuck, at the bike, then back to John.

"Jesus wept, Chuck," he flared. "What do you expect me to do with this ugly piece of shite?" John strode over and smacked the tank contemptuously. That's when it fell over on top of him.

"Watch out for the side stand . . ." Poor Chuck, always a tad too slow.

Red heaved it off John's legs, but not before oil and petrol had spilled down his mac. Surprisingly he didn't jump up and belt whoever was laughing. He just lay there with a surprised expression on his phizog.

"Chuck, you pillock, do you know what you've gotten us into here?"

Chuck looked helplessly at Tinker. Time for introductions, maybe a good time to deal. He reached out and helped John to his feet.

"Tinker's the name, old bikes my game, and this mean ol' lady is a '48 Black Shadow special." He went to pat the tank, then thought better of it. "Despite it just trying to do Chuck in on the way over and kneecaping me, I'd consider taking it off your hands if you're not interested in bikes and the price is right." There were a few posers he would mind seeing on crutches. More than that, however, he wanted to break her in rough, give her stick and put her away wet.

"Well, Tinkerman," John said, "I may know dick about bikes, but this one's more special than you can imagine, and I'm interested." He replaced the fag that got smeared across his face. "Very interested."

Shit, thought Tinker, just when financial prospects were making his knee feel better.

"Hey, don't get your knickers in a knot," John reassured, noting Tinker's long face. "I don't want the bike, I just wanna get something out of it." He turned to Chuck. "C'mon, let's load it up and go to my lock-up. There's a spot of business to attend to before anyone rides off into the sunset."

After unloading at an old warehouse, Red figured he'd better give Shirl a bell to say he'd be late for dinner, and took off to the corner box. Tinker used his chain to lock the Vinnie to a pole before following John and Chuck inside. He didn't bother with the Enfield, the local 'tea leaves' could pinch it for all he cared now. He wanted that big black cat.

John started clearing a big space on the cluttered floor. Tinker thought for the bikes till he started fooling around with a lump of chalk and odd junk from the storage boxes. Bike or no bike, Tinker figured to split when he saw John light up stinking black candles and arrange magic gear around the chalk diagram. He looked at Chuck, and immediately regretted it. He'd begun sweating and trembling like a horse scenting fire. Tinker edged towards the door. Then John spoke over his shoulder.

"You know, it will take more than your chain of faery-bane to keep that bike leashed," he remarked casually. "It's possessed, of course—fascinating case. Usually it's animals or trees, and yet transmigration for sure. Actual metalmorphosis, first I've had my mitts on. Soon as it went for me, I knew." He shrugged. "What a beauty—pity she's gone bad."

Now Tinker had come to horse-trade, not play ghostbusters. Unfortunately the door frame had been filled by Red, and he stared glumly at the intricate layout on the floor.

"Yer at it again, John," he accused. "That bike, she's a wrong 'un, ain't she?" Red looked apologetically at Tinker. "I could feel 'er hating me as I held it down in the back on the way over. I can always smell the rotten eggs."

John puffed a fresh cancer stick into life at a candle. "You always had a good nose, Red, forever sticking it in all the wrong places like me."

Considering Red's once Semitic nose resembled a derailed train, it was a wonder he could smell anything. He flashed a rueful grin. "You should know, you're always leading me by it—charm the foreskin off an elephant you would." He shrugged, then came in. Red never missed a fight.

John turned to Chuck and pulled out the bike papers. "This isn't so much a record of ownership, it's a bloody obituary list. So, playmates, we're gonna stop it right here."

Chuck didn't look too keen on the 'we' idea till John reminded him of the formalities.

"'Course really it's the current owner's problem. He's next." John looked suitably concerned. "Would I be right in thinking this is your signature, Chuck?"

Chuck seemed to nod, 'course it could have been him shaking.

"How's yer knee, Tinkerbell?" John asked. "Is it gonna bend or stand?"

The pain flared up suddenly, blotting out everything else. Yet through the red mist he could still see those eyes, feel John's will forcing him to look.

It was like he re-lived a whole series of bike crashes; experiencing one horrible wreck after another, young men thrown down the road and smashed like eggs. It was always the same bike, the same blood-thirsty laughter. He'd seen their names on the log, yet it was the faces he saw now, and they were all looking at him. Fallen riders; always give a hand to fallen riders—that's the rules.

He met John's stare. "Aye, I'll stand fine."

" . . . and don't go beyond the circle any more than you'd stretch yer hand into a panther's cage."

Tinker cocked a sceptical eye at Red as John rattled on, but only received a hard look that said 'Dummy up and watch yer bottle'.

John took out a penknife and cut away the oil-stained tail of his trench coat. "We're off to the Twilight Zone and no mistake, kiddies. No matter how strange things get, trust in yours truly or we're all up shit creek." The oil-blackened bit of gabardine went into the centre of the penta-wotsit and he bent over it.

Tinker jumped as John deliberately stabbed the blade into his thumb and directed the flow of blood on to the rag, folding the cloth over quickly. Nothing like fresh blood to command attention, and Tinker's drawn to the bright stain as John spread it open again. The crimson blot was in the shape of a corset, like that red leather design on the tank cover.

John lit a fresh coffin nail, took a big drag, then dropped the match on the oily material. He stepped back quickly into the protective concentric rings before it caught.

"We stand at the stations," he intoned, "and have just cause for summoning. You were nearly the death of Chuck here, Tink has a bad limp, my mac's ruined, and . . ." He turned to Red.

"Yeah, Shirl's right pissed," Red grumbled. "Always knows when I'm up to something. Said she's gonna give my steak to the dog.'

"Anyhow," John hurried on, "on behalf on the more serious victims, we call you to account. From the union of my blood with the life fluids of your avatar, I claim the courtesies accorded to kinship. It's show and tell time."

The smouldering rag burst angrily into flame, emitting a foul pall of smoke like a CS canister. Tinker could hardly see across to Red through the greasy black cloud. Whatever could be running in a bike to stink like that, whale oil? Strange, the way it hung there and grew like doom. John went even stranger.

"Now then, don't be shy, Johnny-boy knows what you like." He leered, and took a roughly cut triangle of black leather from his pocket, about the size of a G-string. He held it up to his nose, snuffing and slobbering like pig, then winked suggestively. The seat, Tinker realised. He'd cut out the crotch.

John leaned to the edge of the inner chalk circle, holding it half over, and stretched out an obscene length of tongue. The foul smoke blew in his face like a dust devil and his tongue snapped back faster than a chameleon with a bug—dropping the leather scrap.

It fell half across the chalk line. He stamped down on his side as a high-polished jackboot smoked from out of the cloud on to the other. Tinker nearly swallowed his tonsils, however John spoke with the voice of authority.

"So, we stand toe to toe, yet you cannot cross the fossil dust that has ever barred evil from the world of creation. From the earliest strata of life, her physical remains press you back. The undead may not cross.' He fired Tinker a quick wink. Cocky bastard, you had to like him.

The writhing cloud billowed forward like blood in water. It compressed into a form opposing him, indistinct as a shadow. Unfazed, he blew an enormous smoke ring from lasciviously pouted lips straight into the roiling darkness facing him. It was like an old 'Invisible Man' movie, where steam or powder reveals the features—only they weren't a man's.

A form coalesced, all in black leather with only a pale face showing. Even paler was the platinum hair braided into a thick coif around her head. The Coleridge rhyme came to Tinker ' . . . skin as white as leprosy, the nightmare life-in-death was she . . . ', but it was rage that whitened those pure Aryan cheeks.

"*Untermensch*," she spat, vainly tugging her boot sole against the saddle scrap.

John took a thoughtful drag and flicked away the ash. "Tell you what, speak English and answer my questions. I'll take my foot off your sit-upon."

Lips curled back from sharp, faultless teeth. "Scum!"

"That's me, darlin'," John replied cheerfully, and nudged the fragment over the line. It seemed to flow up the polished boot, like a ripple in black chrome, and lost itself in the flair of tight leather breeches. The tailoring perfection itself; it could have been her own flesh. A military-cut jacket of the same second-skin variety and around the high collar sat a ribbon, on the ribbon a gold swastika within a cog wheel. John hadn't raised any old dominatrix, he'd released a *Valkyrie*.

"Scum," she repeated as if the word was a maggot in her mouth, and she sneered at each of them in turn.

Her finger stabbed out at John. "You, the perverse lunatic."

Chuck quailed before the cold fire of her eyes. "Your quivering dupe, the subnormal."

Tinker on next. "And you, Romany, who would trade me like a horse."

Her eyes were sapphires that hurt to look at. She turned their beam on Red. "Last and lowest of all, *der Jude*, in the foppish guise of a forgotten class to celebrate your decadence. Such kitsch, the tasteless Jew."

Red's face screwed up around his pugilist nose and he slipped out his front dental plate into a velvet-trimmed pocket. He didn't look particularly Jewish. He looked exactly like Winston, his bad tempered bulldog, just before it bit.

"My dad Solly, God bless 'im, fought your blackshirts from Cable Street to Berlin. Nazis don't scare me none."

Unfortunately, nothing did when Red's blood got up, and Tinker realised she must be goading him to break the circle. Luckily, so did John, and he whispered a name.

"*Fraulein* von Schwarzstein."

She spun around like a cat.

"Your name from the motorcycle log." He pulled it from his pocket. "Now you shall give account of yourself in accordance with the rules of naming. You do know they are strictly enforced?"

She hissed hungrily at him, but complied. Tinker stared, fascinated, not every day you learn how to bind a demon.

"General von Schwarzstein was my father. His armoured column got caught refuelling in the Ardennes by rocket-carrying Typhoons during an unlucky break in the weather. He had foreseen the *Gotterdammerung* and made plans. In the event of his death, I'd be smuggled to Argentina where we had relatives. I didn't care what happened to me by then. My Siegfried had also died in that last heroic offensive." Her jaw worked as if anticipating raw flesh. Tinker sure hoped everyone followed the same rule book here.

"Siegfrieg served under Colonel Skorzeny, and had volunteered to deliver false dispatches on a captured American motorcycle. He hit a mine and was found by one of their patrols, wounded and pinned under the machine with his *Schutz Staffel* uniform showing underneath the torn US field jacket. They fired tracer into the petrol tank and roasted him alive like a pig—bragged about it to other prisoners afterwards." She drew coral lips back in a snarl of contempt for lesser breeds. "He had raced *der Kompressor* before the war; none of your effete riders could catch him. He was an iron centaur on that supercharged BMW." Her eyes blazed up like acetylene. "Siegfried died riding for his country. He was a hero, my hero."

Tinker guessed he'd be pure Nordic stock too, nose like a steel ruler and the violent blue eyes of an avenging angel. It dawned on him that this would be her weakness, and potential salvation—good love gone bad. Then the evil rolled thick in her voice again.

"My uncle managed Cimic Ltd. In Buenos Aires, and they had the distributorship for Vincent motorcycles. He obtained the Shadow at my request just before Peron clamped down on imports. Many men have laboured to hone the performance since, yet none had the will to master its power. They all proved weaklings."

Her snarl settled into a thin-lipped smile. "I proved overmatch for the *gaucheros* on their Harley Davidson and Indian carthorses, even the police department's Vincent Rapides were too slow. I ran with the fast set that dabbled in black arts and white powders. Their weakness disgusted me, life disgusted me, only my motorcycle was strong and perfect. It became my shadow, my instrument, my dark desire. Out on the roads at night, we were one, and God help the dawdler that got in our way."

A shockingly red tongue flicked out over cold, perfect lips. "My family had always moved in occult circles. The *Fuhrer's* astrologer became a frequent house-guest and I was considered a promising young student amongst the inner *Reich*. So, as an expatriate ice-blond amongst the greasers, I found judicious applications of sex, money, drugs and blackmail obtained powerful secrets from the self-corrupted. There are old forces that slumber beneath the veneer of civilisation and I discovered how to wake them."

Her laughter rang cruel and hollow. "The Old Ones were strong, ruthless, and hungry. I didn't have to explain my need for revenge, they understood completely. They showed me how to realise my dream. How to become the perfect instrument: no corruptible flesh, no vacillating emotions, a pure killing machine. All it would cost was my worthless life; to finally ride beyond the edge and let my dark steel lover enter this weak vessel. The impact split me wide open; the Old Ones had their blood, and I my will. Now I had become a true *Valkyrie*."

Hell's teeth, thought Tinker. *Talk about the Shadow of Death*. They'd really sucked her into a devil's bargain. It was a terrible black spider John had snared in his web. Mate-less, but sustained for decades on the hot blood of young men who'd striven to master her power—as they did now.

John switched on the charm. Tinker had to admit he was smooth.

"Look, I know what it's like to lose a father, and so many friends and lovers I've lost count. It can really mess your head up. I'm right sorry about what happened; but it was war, and half a century ago. You'll never heal keeping those old wounds open."

You could see John would have his way with the ladies, Tinker wished he could turn on sincerity like a tap.

John spread his hands in a gesture of peace and forgiveness. "It's all over, luv. The *Reich*, Evita and Peron, Vincents—all in the past with the dead. It's time to rest with them now. The killing days are over."

Her nostrils flared in contempt. "You English never change, blind to the forces of manifest destiny, effete and perfidious. My last rider spoke of the Red blunderers crawling to beg for bread at Brandenburg gates. Our time has come again and my country needs me. Only the fittest must survive, and I hunger to thin the *Autobahns* of slave breeds and mud races. Only the best, the strongest, the most pure *Herrenvolk* deserve to live."

Her face looked like something from 'Triumph of the Will', Goebbels had done a great job on this one. How could anyone imagine evil cared which race it fed on? Mind you, Tinker had to allow it did seem partial to the master race. He liked to think there would be a warm place by the fire in Hell for those rarer monsters.

"I thought my new owner would take me back to scour Deutschland clean, but the *bloder kerl* wanted to put me in a museum."

The 'bloody oaf' had five hundred nicker and his life. They had a tiger by the tail. Tinker wet his lips and swallowed. "Hate to tell you, kid, but he's right. You can never go back to the river. They wouldn't let you out of the collection, never mind burning up the *'bahns*. You're not type-approved: too loud, too polluting, too politically incorrect. Really, you'd just be an embarrassment to the new order; they're still trying to pretend people like you never happened."

John picked up on the theme. "S'true, the dead mustn't feed off the quick, so if you won't pass over gracefully, I'll have to exorcise you. All for the best, really." He held out the ownership log close to the candle flame. "Your contract with a Black Shadow; your name, and in your hand. Repent, and let me set you free."

Her laugh was operatic in its range, Wagner would have cried. Every passion was there: sexual challenge, triumph, hatred, and yet . . . torment.

"You don't know me," she hissed. "I am no longer *fraulein* Schwarzstein. Siegfried and I married secretly on his last leave. Father didn't approve of him; not from an aristocratic family, not even in the party. Yet he was the man for me—nobody rode like Siegfried. He lived decent and pure as I am now evil. He would have forgiven even those who took him from me, but not I. They widowed me—*und jetz Ich bin die Schwarzwitwe!*"

Jesus, Tinker thought, remembering a smattering of school German. *She is and all.* The Black Widow, and he'd thought it was just another motorcycle apocrypha. He'd heard about the ghost Vincent that rode its riders to death but somehow always survived to kill again. The Stevenage factory made Shadows, Lightnings, Knights and Princes, all of them Black. Tinker had always assumed some joker made up that Black Widow story: he wasn't laughing any.

She curled her lip, and spat. John's candle went out.

The cigarette butt fell from nerveless fingers. That candle had been on their side of the line. She pointed a buffed black toe at where John had pushed the scrap of leather over to her. The suede side had wiped a path through the chalk!

Time slowed down like in a bike crash. The blood left John's face, Chuck groaned, and Red tensed to spring. Absolutely nothing Tinker could do: nada, nix, zilch. Memory pounded for attention. *Zilch? Zilcher? Zilcher, best of the Kompressor riders before the war. Wasn't his initial S?* Perhaps it wouldn't be Tinker's day to die after all.

"*Frau* Zilcher," he whispered gently. Nothing falls harder on the ear of a demon than its true name.

She whipped around with a hiss—what a face! Beauty and naked horror, so deadly dangerous, yet so vulnerable. It had fallen on him to pronounce sentence.

Tinker lips moved again, yet the voice wasn't his own.

"*Liebschen.*"

She froze, eyes opening wide. Looking right through him, she took a step forward. "Siegfried?"

Then a fiery explosion blew in the door, knocking them down like ninepins. Dazed, they picked themselves up and rushed outside. The Vinnie was a pillar of hungry flame and, standing beside it smelling of singed peroxide, stood Shirley.

"Okay, where's that fancy leather girl you were ogling?" she shrilled at Red. "She won't get far without her bike, and when I catch . . ." Shirl stopped in mid-screech, and they followed her eyes. In the flames stood the terrible answer.

The Widow was burning with her bike. Blazing petrol had stripped away the leathers and underneath the blistering, peeling skin hid evil incarnated in steel—the metalmorph! Tinker flashed on Bridgette Helm as the insane robot, Maria, burned at the stake in Fritz Lang's 'Metropolis'. They all gaped and stepped back. The heat waxed and the alloy parts were going Salvador Dali. Then, as if a movie in reverse, pink virgin flesh lay under the molten metal that rolled off her flanks in toxic, glittering beads. Yet it wasn't the body of a Brunnhilde the incandescence revealed. She was a girl, fresh in the first blush and innocence of youth. Her face uplifted to a brighter light, eyes far focussed and lips parted in wonder.

"*Mein* Siegfried," she whispered. "*Ich komt.*"

Then there was only the stink of burning rubber and metallic smoke catching at their throats. The bike had become a puddle of slag, and John held the log over its dwindling flames, using it to light a fag before dropping it into the embers.

"Forget that five hundred quid, Chuck," he muttered. "I reckon we all got our money's worth."

Red and Shirl made up, and nipped off home for a quickie. John put the 'fluence on Chuck to stop him flipping out and stuffed him in the van. He followed Tinker over to his bike. The tyres seemed unmelted and the paint hadn't bubbled. Somewhere a beer started calling for Tinker by name.

"Did good in there, wack," said John. "Got the gift, you have. Siegfried knew you were the best conduit." A visiting card appeared in his fingers and got tucked under the goggles strap. "Could be the start of a beautiful relationship."

That'd be right, thought Tinker, riding home. *In a rain of pig's puddings.*

The little Enfield didn't seem too slow at all. Stands to reason, meeting a bike widow always puts you off burn-ups.

HARD IAIN

Hard Ian was a right bastard, and a mongrel at that. His mother a full-blood Indian who died when he was two, his father a Milwaukee Yank who later took up with a Jap. Funny how it goes. Wouldn't call Ian a giant, but lots of muscle and no fat. Despite being past the big Five-O, his stamina would still shame young 'uns. He was full of tricks, and created, like the Frankenstein monster, out of odd bits.

Tinker's resurrections didn't shape up tricky though. Old bikes were his trade, the odder the better as long as they had soul, which Ian had in spades. Oh, you could call Ian a bastardised bike all right; a bit of this, a bit of that.

Iain, on the other hand. Now he were a bit of the other.

It happened that Tinker languished without wheels when a mate called with a problem. Seemed the used Harley Evolution motor he'd obtained for his rigid chop project had turned out to be hotter than a Chernobyl jockstrap. The plod were coming and he figured they would seize the lot for evidence, or more likely for ever. He'd decided to part out the bits cheap and fast. Tinker never touch stolen parts on principle and tended to leave custom hogs to others who had less sensitive fingers. Still, the 'six into four' transmission and aftermarket chassis were legit. Besides, he already had an '51 eighty-inch Bonneville Chief engine camped under the workbench next to a chrome Sport Scout girder front end. Always ready to help a friend in need, especially if the price might be right.

So, he ended up with a mongrel. A gypsy and his dog, you might say, and every dog has to have a name. It had been Magic John that taught him the importance of naming, 'course that gutter mage knew as much about bikes as Tinker did the Grimorium.

Tinker cut up two sets of tank transfers and grafted a half-set of HD wings on to the Indian war bonnet like a Viking or that Ogri 'toon. Shuffling the Harley/Indian lettering around produced 'Indley', but that only suggested car racing and walnut veneer dashes. Then he thought of the 'Vindian', a blue-ribboned bastardization if ever there was one. The Stevenage Vincent factory stuffed their Rapide powerplant into a Chief chassis. Looked great, however it was like going from the helm of a yacht to the Queen Mary according to Phil Irving, Vincent's top designer. It sure frightened the shit outta the local plod when it blasted past at over the ton. American barges never impressed the Brits. Still, it got Tinker to thinking, how about 'Hardian'?

So that was how 'Hard Ian' got his name, but there is always more to it than that. It seems that when you hand-make a cycle of desire the Pygmalion effect kicks in, and frequently its reverse with Philistines. Nobody cares about the mass-produced junk, however tank art and personal names are a statement that invite comment. Now you couldn't call Tinker a fighting man, but he figured to stand behind Ian when the slaggers moved in. He didn't have to wait long.

For starters the wimps said the bike looked too Spartan. These were the spinal fusion, bum grapes, dribbly kidneys and swingy arm association. Buncha nancy-boys, as far as he cared.

"Only good for pub to pub," they'd whine. Yeah, that'd be right, he put on more miles in a month than they'd had hot dinners.

"You'll break your back/frame/the law etc." This from blokes who wouldn't notice if their Gold Wing retirement home sprouted extra wheels. Only the anally disabled needed rear suspension these days; with the advent of pogo seats, balloon tyres, and decent blacktop, who ever did? Tinker preferred the direct sensation of a rigid any day. 'What's the matter, softie-tail, frightened you might feel something?' Able-bodied men actually shook their heads over the magneto and kicker combination. 'Wot, no electric leg? Won't start right.' Right away, every time.

Everybody, of course, picked on the open belts. 'Catch yer jeans in there f'sure.' Sure, if he was still wearing bell bottoms into the millennium. You can't fully enclose a rear, and front aramid belts tend to snap from the heat if they aren't open for ventilation. Besides, plenty old bikes ran semi-open primary chains; still do for vintage racing and never a chewed ankle.

The tank art really caused the grief though. The proposed Chief head/HD wing montage started looking awful familiar to a certain outlaw club associate. Offending the briar 'n belstaff jacket boys is one thing, but patch holders take a dim view of copyright infringement. Kind of view you'd get from the bottom of a flooded quarry as you lie zpped inside a sleeping bag with a concrete block for company.

After the hurried paint-over, a last umpteenth coat of epoxy clear dried over what had been the Chief's face. Now a savage stared out from beneath a rage of limed-up hair, even a torc and wode-blue tattoos. It was the bike's personality asserted its character on those tanks, not the artist's. The face had come to Tinker, he awoke from a dream with it still imprinted on his eyes. Hard Ian could only be a Pict warrior.

Predictably, he proved a monster, only part-broken by modern brakes and Super Venom tyres. Scary at speed in rutted corners, heroic on hills, and bags of hairy chested power up to about 5,000 rpm after which the flathead swirl-effect started losing its claim to efficient breathing. Of course much over the ton and Tinker started breathing pretty heavy too.

A sprinkling of RUB on a Softail Hog was porridge to Ian though. He'd have 'em for breakfast. Pretty soon the local scoffers put-up or shut-up, and Ian earned a reputation as a mean bike. Tinker earned his grey hairs just hanging on.

It had been Magic John as told him that Ian, or more correctly Iain, was Scots Gaelic for John; like Sean in Ireland. Originally the name John itself from the Hebrew Johanan, 'the favoured of Jehovah'. Mind you, the Baptist must have had his doubts when Salome started cranking up her lust-sacrifice ritual—make a few men lose their heads that would.

John is everywhere: Jan in Holland, Jean in France, Ivan in Russia, Evan in Wales, Juan, Giovanni . . . and of course plain old Jack. Jack would always be climbing up beanstalks, falling down hills; or as Iain fancied himself, being a giant killer. High-performance plastic punks galled him at their peril. With a five gallon capacity, overdrive sixth, and Iain's hand on the tap, he'd catch up with them eventually.

So, Hard Iain was also Iron John, or properly *Eisen* Hans from the Grimm's collection of folk legends. The male mentor who accepted you on his back and took to trial through the ways of the world. Yeah, that would be Iain. He'd been Iain to Tinker from the first time they hit the road—Iain the iron man.

Tinker's supposed pal, Magic John, had looked long into the glistening fat-bob tanks and Iain had stared unblinking back. Those hawk-like features weren't from just one race anymore than a gypsy like Tinker. Haida raiding dugout or Viking longship would call this face captain, and you could argue that the early central Asian horsemen who became Celt charioteers, saw their final flowering on the staked plains of the Comanche under such a Chief.

"What you got here," John said in that cheerful tone Tinker had come to associated with a friend's misfortunes, "is an old ancestor with a hero complex, typically on the large and simple side. Sorta like those punchy boxers that don't know the bell has tolled for them."

Tinker told him it was only a bike, but didn't believe that either. He well knew some bikes become vehicles for lost souls. "C'mon John," he reasoned. "I'm not really a cafe cowboy, me and the bike are too old for that hero stuff."

John looked skeptically at the blued pipes and scraped-down footrests. "You're just lucky it's not channelling one of those kamikaze speed demons going around. Lotta punks being sacrificed on an altar of Jappo technology." He shook his head. "Nobody ever believes in demonic possession till it's too late. Anyhow, this one is okay; symbiotic and 100% organically home-grown. He just wants to fuck and fight, to race chariots and swill the mead out of life's endless horn again. It should be quite a ride while it lasts."

Tinker didn't care much for that 'while it lasts' bit, and didn't think John was referring to the bike's mechanical integrity.

Iain came on wild as the North Wind that blew down from the Grampians and over the walls of Emperors. Sometimes he looked like a pagan Mercury, hair spiked up and blown back, lime-white against the jet storm cloud of the five gallon teardrop tanks. Went like the wind too, until he ran out of it at about ton-twenty, could run wide-open all day mind you. Old iron isn't meant to be able to do that.

He made Tinker remember things best forgotten by a respectable classic dealer in his middle years. Little things like the trembling of a young girl pasted to your back, high speed pursuit, and hospital food. Things like coming down hard on the kicker and burning out of a pub lot with a swelling left fist and only a fragmented action replay of blood, flying teeth. Kind of odd—not only was Tinker non-violent by inclination and ability, but also right-handed. Maybe Leonardo could bend iron bars sinistral, but as a punch-out artist Tinker felt more the wimpy Robert Crumb-type. So where did that coil-spring, straight left flash from? Neither he nor its victims knew till it was too late.

John just laughed when asked. "After all, Tinker," he gloated. "It's only fair. You get to ride him, and sometimes Iain gets to ride you."

Things came to a head at the International V-Twin Rally in Hereford. Tinker had just started carving out a choice portion of tenderloin from the pig roast when this gigantic Italian decided he had prior claim.

"Moto Guzzi she is the best V-twin and we take over this rally now. Only the best for us, Indian-lover," he bragged reaching over to take Tinker's plate.

Heard the one about 'What does a 500lb gorilla eat?' Well, this monster stood like an extra from one of those old Steve Reeves spaghetti 'n beefcake epics; even the Harley riders were turning a deaf 'un and just muttering into their beer.

Did Iain care about big? He took Tinker's tongue.

"Your Caesar Carcano copied the Indian 841 shaft-drive for his 'mechanical mule'. That was the first transverseV-twin Guzzi—no forked tongue to say your bike's mother was a donkey."

Everybody within earshot froze.

"Indian made the 841 for the North African desert campaign," Tinker's lips continued to blurt, "Unfortunately they never got much action because your legions ran away when they saw them coming. Musso's boys were only good at gassing spear-chuckers anyhow."

Tinker froze, alas too late. Iain had got in-the-face, and there would be a fight. Guilo Carcano's middle name was Cesar, he designed their V-8 racer and was virtually a god-emperor to Guzzi fanatics.

Hercules here went the colour of Chianti and drew back a fist like Jove's thunderbolt. A boot blade flashed in Tinker's hand as Iain spoke again.

"Hold you, Ro-man, in my tribe the cut of meat is settled at the knife."

Iain's hands tore the bandanna from Tinker's neck and clamped teeth down on one end, holding out the other. "Pull the stiletto out of your sleeve where we can all see it, and take a bite on this so you can't be sneaking up behind me—I've heard about Italian habits. Besides, it'll stop you teeth chattering."

Tinker could neither hold his tongue nor the lips that writhed back in Iain's contemptuous snarl. "If you have the liver to fight, I'll season my cut with your gall."

Part of him screamed to shut the fuck up and run like hell, but the other coolly contemplated the prospect of this head in a box of cedar oil as an after-dinner conversation piece. That would be the part the Itie saw beckoning in his eyes and singing along the bowie's edge.

"You a crazy man," he muttered, backing off rapidly. "I don't got no knife. Eat pig, eat shit. I no care."

"Your sort were only good in a cohort, man to man we carved you like capons," Iain grunted, then ignored him and tucked the bandanna back under Tinker's chin. "Be off with you now before you turn the meat yellow."

He might as well have, Tinker could barely get it down after Iain got out of the saddle and the adrenalin reaction set in. Still, it's an ill wind—he couldn't buy a single beer all night. Word got about and the Hogsters got in the rounds. He even found favour in the admiring eyes of a lycra-clad lady after they closed down the beer tent. Funny how Iain had that effect on people, for sure Tinker never did.

He lay sleeping like an egg when an explosion occurred, followed by the roar of flames. Tinker jumped up bollock-naked.

"My bike!"

He could see it through the tent like a fuckin' X-ray. Then movement in the flames, and screaming. The dirty Wop had torched Iain, yet seemed caught in the conflagration. Burning like a Wickerman and flailing around with his jacket cuff caught on the controls. The more he struggled, the more blazing petrol sloshed out. Then the bike fell over, pinning him down.

They burned together, and no one could get near them—Tinker didn't even try. Iain would have liked it this way: a foe immolated on his funeral pyre after a night of boar, beer, and babes.

Oh, there wouldn't be a problem with the insurance payout; plenty of witnesses and the coroner would record 'death by misadventure'.

Tinker rode away on the arsonist's Guzzi Mark IV 1000S. His by right, and no one said a dickybird.

Days later, Tinker could still see Iain's face through the flames. The transfer crinkling up in a fiery grin as the pyre roared with his wild laughter—then he was gone. Or so Tinker thought—till the next fight.

FREE RIDE

Tinker was feeling pretty chipper: bank balance in the black and a few choice rides stashed against a rainy day: his health, freedom, and a couple of pints of 'Old Peculiar' marinating the lunchtime pork pie and pickles. The Harley KHK was doing what it liked best too, burbling along with a busy side-valve clatter. Just when he was thinking life couldn't get much better, it did.

He came around a corner, and there she stood with her thumb out for a ride. Even if she'd been old and ugly, he'd have stopped. They were in the middle of Lower Nowhere, nothing but fallow ground for miles and no other traffic that he'd noticed.

Tinker turned in the saddle as she came running up. Harley brakes aren't really that bad, he just liked to see a woman hurrying towards him with a smile on her face.

She bounced up. "Wow, neato! I just love motorcycles."

Miss Jailbait-of-the-Month talked even younger than she looked and was built like a bird. A little blackbird in punk feathers setting off her unseasonable pallor. Pretty with it, however far too cheerfully innocent for even a hardened molester, let alone him.

Tinker popped the lid off a teardrop saddlebag and hauled out his spare half-helmet; a handy minimum-compliance accoutrement for single gentlemen with empty pillions.

"Sorry, luv. You'll have to wear this. The State sits up nights figuring out new laws to safeguard the health of tearaways on bikes." He passed it over and their fingers 'accidentally' brushed. *Jeez*, he thought, *must have a warm heart for hands that cold.* Make that bad heart; there was a cyanotic tinge around her black-painted lips and circulation problems might account for that pallid skin too.

She set the helmet at a jaunty angle and checked her new millinery in the mirror. What a little minx, with his luck she'd probably be the Chief Constable's medically-fragile only child. He felt mildly relieved that she even had a reflection, he had to be so careful these days. Hanging with Magic John seemed to invite strange company—sleep with tramps, wake with fleas.

She hopped on behind with a squeal of delight, and he shrugged away caution. 'Great bait if you're fishing for men' as the angler said of the vicar's pretty daughter.

They were just taking off when he felt her rise up on the rear pegs and turn. "You sure you're okay?" Tinker asked suspiciously. Impaired or neurotic passengers can be lethal.

"Oh, don't mind me, I'm fine," she giggled. "I'm only waving so my friends will see me riding by."

Huh? thought Tinker. There wasn't so much as a sheep in sight, just a rough field with a prominent bump in the middle. He twisted around to see what was up. She was waving in the direction of that odd-shaped hillock. *Hmm.* He slowed down and made a partial switch into his gypsy second sight, about all he'd inherited from a runaway dad. Age-worn shades of men stood there, rippling like torn shadows in a silent wind and waving swords. Of course, that mound was a barrow tomb, the pendant digging into his back was an *Ankh*, and his punkette passenger pale and cold as . . . Instinctively Tinker's hand clutched at his chest.

"Muvver!" Well, what would anyone's last words be? He was a practising pagan, and in times of mortal fear, quite good at it. Mother was the Willendorf Venus pendant he wore. An original, and a whole other story about how he came by her. Magic has a way of hanging around your neck like a stone.

Good old mum. She radiated warmth and life into his heart to counter the deathly cold claiming his back. Tinker was caught in the moment between life-maker and taker. It felt twixt the rock and hard place. Rail-thin arms encircled him and he near gave up for lost. One of those inexplicable single-vehicle fatalities no-one can account for. She must have felt him stiffen, and not where a girl might expect.

"Going my way, Tinker?" she whispered in his ear, and nearly had them both in the ditch. She laughed in delight as he wrestled nerves and buckhorn bars back under control. "It's okay, honest. Cross my heart and hope to . . . Well, anyway, today's my day off, only silly old Sol never takes a break. Let's say a mutual friend suggested we go for a ride."

So, he wasn't going to be bench-pressing the buttercups with the barrow-wights. The air suddenly seemed sweeter, the light more vibrant. Even the bike smoothed out and Death didn't seem so cold or too young. Today wasn't his day to be popping the clogs after all.

The faster he rode, the better she liked it. Hey, a snappy bike, a pretty girl, and a perfect day to be immortal. When Death promises she isn't pulling your number, you can get away with murder. After all, could say it wouldn't be the first time he'd ridden with the Reaper at his shoulder, and she had asked for a ride. The rules of magic were immutable and universal—ask a favour, incur a debt.

"Ah, my lady Death, can I be taking you anywhere special?" Receiving no reply he tried again. "Going far, are we?". He caught her frown in the mirror and hurried on. "Not that I'm anything less than enchanted with your company."

Some of the chill returned. "Oh, you big liar. Life is never comfortable around me, it's a mother and daughter thing."

His Venus pendant twitched in irritated acknowledgement. Like he needed being in the middle of a family spat. Fortunately, they came to a crossroads, and she pointed sharp left.

"That way," she said. "There's an old friend of mine you really ought to meet, then I won't be beholding to John for this get-together. He's forever moaning on about how I'm always taking his friends." Death paused, then giggled. "Oh, I don't mean you. Still, it's hardly surprising really, the stuff he gets them into."

Tinker could give bloody Magic John a few tips about how to keep them right now. He wondered just how old this friend of hers was—she heard, of course.

"Oh," she tittered behind her hand. "Anarch is even older than . . . than me," she finished, then fell silent.

He caught her checking in the mirror for wrinkles as they came up to a small pub. *Ha, Death be not proud.*

Without instruction, his hands guided them into the car park. They wouldn't let go the bars for less than a pint pot apiece under the circumstances. Great, there was another bike there already; hopefully that meant they served bikers.

A metal 'No Motorcycle Parking' sign appeared to have been crumpled up and used as a urinal. Hopefully there would be a hard-arse horny biker Tinker could somehow dump grave-bait on. He walked over to the bike with Death, hoping to praise its superior qualities. Wrong! It had an moth-eaten blanket for a saddle and no mudguards or brakes. No lighting equipment or license plate either. However, it did have a supercharger and it was a S. S.

100 Brough. Black as a starless night, stripped to the bone, twin magnetos, and two-inch diameter straight-through pipes.

Christ! Tinker thought, *it must sound like a B-36 bomber.* Who could get away with riding a mother-fucking monster like that?

"Death!" A stentorian bellow emanated from a vast black beard and the better part of two cowhides occluding light from the pub doorway. "Who's the wimp?"

Now normally that would be fighting talk, but Mr. Anarch here was one big daddy. He unhooked thick welder's glasses and weird eyes flicked over Tinker dismissively. They glittered like black pearls beneath the bushy shadows of his brow, no whites at all. They didn't even look like eyes, more holes down into nothingness. It took real effort for Tinker to tear his gaze away.

"Suppose you'd better come in then," he said, replacing the goggles. "Gargle is on me."

"Ooh, I'd love a Babycham," Death cooed, gazing sweetly up into his hairy scowl.

Now Tinker would drink with the Devil as long as he was buying. He nodded: Anarch ignored him. Tinker felt his temper stir and knew he'd be heading for trouble.

No surprise to find the bar deserted. The landlord would probably be either still running, or locked himself in his cellar. On the other hand, Anarch could have eaten him.

"I suppose the pansy here will want fizz too," Anarch muttered, thumbing off a cap.

Before Tinker could push him down, Iain had his tongue. Terrible pride, had Iain, and knew fear no better than soap and water—typical Pict. Iain being Tinker's inner warrior, an ancestor who'd vectored into him via a possessed bike. Tinker hadn't the heart to exorcise him. Unfortunately he constituted a chronic liability if you were allergic to involuntary confinement or hospital food.

"Stick the ale-horn up your arse, blanket-rider." The worst Pictish contempt was reserved for saddles, made for men with female parts as they put it.

The colossus turreted around with a wild twinkle in those hard vacuum eyes that sparked through the shades—bit like Ernest Borgnine in 'The Vikings'. "Why, if it isn't young Iain. Can't say much for the horse you rode in on." His hands came up like excavator buckets. "Don't you know it's rude to crash a private party?"

Now Iain had to be near a couple of thousand years old and died at least twice to Tinker's knowledge. Luckily it didn't seem he was up for thirds, and Iain suffered himself to be stuffed back into the red-branching depths of Tinker's gut. It didn't seem as if he was backing down, more like acknowledging fealty. At any event, Tinker got a pint of wallop out of the exchange and Anarch quit calling him a wimp.

Damn, he sure looked like Hemingway in his early Key West days. The same great expanse of beard over a massive chest, but Tinker couldn't get over those eyes. Like miners' expectorate in snow; black as sin, and all the way down. If he recalled his Milton, Anarch predated creation. Hey, what existed before Khaos?

Death giggled as the cheap Babycham bubbles got up her nose. If it hadn't been for Magic John's description he'd never have twigged this was the infamous Grim Reaper. Anarch, however, was clearly a maniac of the first water, and from his expression felt it had brewed better beer. He'd been mixing Wee Heavies with Stingo, and still grumbling about never having had decent brew since Uruk, wherever that was. Anarch slipped a battered silver flask out of his jacket to boost the tankard's octane. He nodded a silent offer in Tinker's direction, and chuckled over his hasty demurring.

'Accept no favours from the Fey, especially spirits,' John had warned him. Like Tinker needed to get deeper into the morass of magic. Anarch's *potheen* would probably be equal parts nitroglycerine and adrenochrome, and even receiving the offer created a burden. John had said the secret was to make a proposition the other party couldn't refuse. Great, but what did Tinker have that Anarch could possibly want?

Then it came to him, what do oldsters value above memories? He searched for a remembrancer. Maybe the Brough pin on his tatty leather riding vest. Nah, too obvious. The vest was like Technicolour scale mail with all the lost marque pins and causes, there had to be something. How about an 'Eat the Rich' button? Nope, Anarch probably had already. Tinker's fingers fumbled to the rescue. An original CNT/FAI enamel pin, its diagonally divided scarlet and black the borderlines of Spain's bloody civil war. It had been about all that came back from uncle Bill after he left with the International Brigade. He died fighting for POUM, a family hero.

Tinker pushed it across the table to Anarch and saw his fingers twitch.

"*Confederacion Nacional Trabjo*," he whispered to himself, lost in memory as he reached out to touch it. "*Federacion Anararquisto Iberica*. Buenaventura Durruti."

Tinker had read the story of Durruti in an old 'Anarchy' underground comic, the artist's penname was Spain. Durruti, the proletarian hero of Bill's infrequent letters from the front where both had died So many brave dreamers, all but forgotten now.

Anarch held the pin before his eyes, where a mist seemed to have formed on the lenses. "*No pasaran*," he challenged to fascists in general, Franco in particular.

"They shall not pass," Tinker agreed fervently. It had been the defiant slogan of besieged Madrid, where Durruti's funeral turned out the whole population. Tinker wished he'd been there; Anarch obviously had.

Whew, Tinker relaxed. *Gorra know how to handle chthonic elementals.* Tempermentals more like. Powerful big, yet susceptible to emotional ju-jitsu.

"Oh, I just knew you two would get along," Death squealed, clapping her hands. "I know, let's have a toast. These are on me."

As if by magic, what else? Three terracotta beakers appeared before them, moisture beading on the cuneiform embossed clay. Anarch lifted his and sniffed appreciatively. "Best Sumerian temple brew. Mmm, been a long time." He emptied his flask into the beaker.

Now Tinker would quaff old ale with the best, however five thousand years was pushing shelf-life a tad. They tapped pots and Anarch proposed the toast.

"Death . . . your pardon, my lady." She inclined her head graciously. "Death to order."

Tinker could drink to that. *Here goes nothing*, he thought, and tipped it back. His eyes bulged, that stuff could make the Sphinx pass a pyramid. If it had fuelled the artisans of Babel, small wonder they ended up talking funny.

"Hello, hello, and what's all this then?"

Talking of funny turns, here came the local plod displaying his impeccable sense of timing.

"We don't want your sort hanging around here," he snapped peevishly. "On yer bikes."

Anarch's face took on that Ragnar Lothbrok expression again and his lips curled back in a wicked grin. Sensing a fight, Iain began hammering on the hatch too.

"Now boys," Death cautioned, "remember it's my holiday."

"And just who might you be, missy?" Constable Tired-of-Life demanded. "You don't even look old enough to be drinking."

"But officer," she wheedled, radiating youthful innocence, "We're not drinking bad stuff. Here, taste it if you don't believe me." Her pout was most convincing.

Oh no, Tinker groaned inwardly as the luckless sap raised the beaker to his lips. It was Anarch's she passed him.

The poor bastard hit the floor as if an embalmer had whipped out his skeleton.

Anarch threw back his head and laughed mightily. "Fine girl you are, Death," he spluttered around a big swig of copper's folly. "Never did like uniformed piss-sippers."

"It won't kill him, will it?" Death didn't sound too pleased.

"Mother's milk," chortled Anarch. "Not that she'd suckle a runt like him."

"Er, what would be in that flask exactly?" Tinker asked, relieved to have passed on the offer.

"Why, spirits of liberty of course, silly." Death shook her head at his ignorance.

Tinker looked down at the unfortunate son of Robert Peel. Pissed the blue serge pants and face the colour of a meths drinker on antabuse. A touch of foam bubbled at the corners of his idiotically smiling lips—totally gonzo! His legs twitched like a dog after dream hares and fly buttons strained behind a whopping erection. Boy, wait till the sergeant came looking and found him all fucked-up on duty like this.

They decided not to bother waiting. He wasn't much company and the reek of piss had put a damper on things. Outside they were figuring their separate ways when Anarch started getting antsy. He scratched in his unruly hair and shuffled from one size twenty to another before getting it out.

"Thing is, I'm in your debt, *companero*," he admitted, touching the pin. It stood out like a drop of fresh blood against the black of his leathers. "I can't leave till you give me a chance to make it right. Ask for anything."

Ah ha! So some rules bound Mr. Anarchy himself. Tinker looked at Death. Even she had gone thoughtful.

"Are you still on holiday?" Tinker asked, feeling lucky.

"Till the stroke of midnight," she confirmed.

Big breath. "Well, in that case I'll take the Brough."

Anarch looked fit to burst, and Death broke up in peals of girlish laughter. *Right*, thought Tinker. *Now laugh this off.*

"So, my lady, I've no seat for you now and I can't be riding two bikes at once. You'll have to take my bike. Remember, you did ask me for a ride in the first place." He forced himself to look in her eyes. "See, I can hardly put Anarch back in my debt by asking him to take it and I don't suppose you're familiar with handling old iron. So he'll have to play *chauffeur* or you'll both be stranded here."

Beat that for snookering, John. Tinker smiled. Death takes the Harley and the big guy has to deliver. They both ride out of his life, and Tinker would be invulnerable till the witching hour. He had the spirit-horse of a premortal and Death owed him a hog-sized favour, a big one. That wasn't just any old '55 KHK, once upon a time, it had belonged to a king—well, of rock 'n roll, Death would remember him. Yes, Tinker had struck worse deals.

They looked good together, riding away. Freedom and Death often share the same saddle. *Everybody happy? Right.*

Tinker turned to the Brough and flexed his fingers. "Now, you and me are going for a little ride."

Tinker awoke in the dark with a king-hell brain pain. The stink of antiseptic invaded his nostrils, and . . . cigarettes?

He forced open swollen eyes and groaned. John, pulling a 'Bogeyman' impersonation in the upflare of his hard-drawn fag.

"Wotcher, Tink," he said in the usual malicious tones, yet with a hint of concealed concern. Probably wondering where he would get another sucker if Tinker snuffed it. John always had problems keeping friends—alive, that is.

"Where am I?" Tinker managed to croak through split lips.

"Emergency. Hey, you gave us all a good scare. The quacks say you got no business being alive, me old mate." John took another drag and tutted over the chart. "Just as well I'm looking after you, kiddo. You got a lot to learn before you go cocking your leg with the big dogs."

Tinker groaned aloud as shrapnel-fragments of memory returned. Anarch must have slipped some of that liberty hooch into his beer because Tinker didn't normally challenge all-comers out on the road, especially ones with blinky lights. It must have been some ride while it lasted. He sure hoped when he recalled the details it would be worth how he felt now. No more Sumerian coffin-rattler for him.

"Thought I'd better come and spring you, if you're up to it," John continued. "The motorway fuzz are waiting outside to talk to you most severely. Something about repeatedly provoking high-speed pursuit, unsafe vehicle, no helmet and indecent exposure. They expect the blood tests back any minute to confirm controlled substances."

Another, louder groan from Tinker. "Can you get me home before midnight? I'd sooner die in my own bed than this butcher's shop."

"Die, die?" He laughed softly. "Oh no, you're not going to be that lucky. Death can't go around taking out her creditors, it's terribly bad form. So, no more simple life for you, chummy, nobody likes grave-cheaters. Hell, I should know." He got his arms under Tinker's shoulders and heaved. "Bit unfair, really, it's not like we don't suffer the same, eh?"

Tinker bit down hard and lurched to his feet feeling every particle of pain. No argument here.

Chuck, John's fridge bulb-brained buddy, sat waiting in the back alley with his van. A bike lay inside with bent Castle forks and scraped tanks reflecting the sodium street lamps like burnished coal.

"Thanks, John," Tinker gritted past clenched teeth. Even getting in was a blur of agony. "I owe you one."

"Don't sweat it, sonny boy," he reassured. "You've got all the time in the world to work it off—as my apprentice, that is. You're gonna need training once the word gets out there's a new player, can't afford to bungle in jungle.'

"Maybe you're right on this one, John," Tinker mumbled through the pain. "I guess there's no such thing as a free ride."

PICTOGLYPH

"Bonnie bloody Scotland," Tinker cursed to himself. "Aye, between the raindrops."

An overpass on the A90 lent a brief respite from the downpour as he struggled into his black, one-piece rain suit over wet leathers. He looked like a man wrestling his shadow.

In a way, he was. The shade of Iain, a long-dead Pictish ancestor, lurked in his guts like a symbiotic tapeworm. Ghosts and tapeworms were always getting mistaken for demons back then. Tinker's sorcerer apprenticeship to the best gutter-mage in Britain obviously included the casting out of demons, but Iain was old family. They shared the same coal-black curls and disconcerting green eyes, exercise-hardened thews and independent nature. Neither had much time for tick-tock men or their concrete concentration camps. They agreed on little else.

Tinker's stomach lurched, and it wasn't the dodgy scotch egg or the slightly sour pint from lunch.

"Look, Iain," he muttered in exasperation. "The stones have been standing nearly two thousand years and you giving me the shits in a zipped-up rainsuit isn't going to speed things up right now." Picts and patience never sat at the same table, and Iain had been waiting a couple of millennia for this tour.

If someone had told Tinker that he'd be freezing through 'scotch mist' instead of being all toasty at the Portugal rally in Faro as planned . . . ! Well, when that someone is Iain and the usual lures of cheap drink and naked women, shared with wild tribes of iron-horsemen, fails to entice a warrior Pict—you must succumb to the inevitable.

"The stones are calling," Iain had stated one morning, rumbling like a bad curry. And that was that.

"Worse than being married," Tinker grumbled to himself, for the umpteenth time. However, the rain was past and surprisingly the big Vee had not missed a beat all day. Hours of back roads to nowhere pulling second gear through stone-walled twisties wasn't really this American freeway-burner's cup of fifty-weight. Blasting south through France with an ever-warmer wind in Tinker's hair would have suited both far better.

"Just sort it out for me, Tinker?" the high-roller owner had said, pointing to the great lump of finned alloy leaking oil in his trailer. "I don't have the time and I don't want it showing me up. I hear you're magic with special bikes."

Tinker was half-gypsy, horse trading a family tradition, and old or odd artefacts his day job. He'd heard about these automotive derived V-twins; a great concept using only Chevy V-8 engine parts but ruined by careless execution. Everything would have to be torn down and 'blueprinted' to proper specs, then road tested. Tinker decided he needed the grief less than the moolah, besides he didn't like whoring a decent ride for poseurs.

"Make it worth your while," said Mr. Deep Pockets.

Tinker shrugged, unconvinced.

Deep Pockets told him how much worth. He had rough friends.

Reluctantly, Tinker reached for the dash switch and the ninety-degree pulse ceased. It had become his reassuring constant in a rough day, but it was the end of the road now.

Needless to say nothing had pleased Iain. The big relief-carved stone in Aberlemno had been a hit, until he saw the big Celtic cross on the reverse. Pagan Pict to the bone and xenophobic to anything new and foreign, he especially shied from 'Ro-man diseases' caught in the near east. It had taken a couple of bottles of Fraoch heather ale to settle him down.

Avoiding the later Christianised stones, Tinker had taken his live-in ancestor from ruined churchyards, each obviously built around their stone, to typically ghastly council estates with bloody great ogham-engraved monoliths looking like they'd fallen there from outer space. Unfortunately, churches gave Iain the creeps and cities made him claustrophobic. Battle scenes, wild hunts, and cryptic symbol stones standing in the middle of muddy fields he liked—they reminded him of his childhood.

Then there was that endless first gear meandering up in the raw hills around the vitrified hill forts at Catterthun. Iain wanted to visit Mons Grampus; *mons veneris* held more appeal for Tinker, but Iain had to pay respects at the ancient battle site. Trouble was both Romans and Picts had forgotten its location, and Iain had only been a boy brought along for the accuracy of his slingshot. It had proved a coming-of-age; alas, a new one.

"The cowards fought but to win," Iain cursed, sniffing the air. "No champions, martial displays, or even eloquent braggings. We might as well have thrown ourselves against your machines." Iain had seen the future at Mons Grampus, and known fear.

Up and down every farm lane and footpath. The Vee grew hot, and Tinker hotter plodding through the heather around the two ruined forts. For compensation there was a fine view as the sun headed towards the west, gilding the distant rolling fields of barley and softening endless moors as they sloped upwards into the great swelling Grampians.

Iain dragged him through rock and bog, but eventually had to give up. "I was watching our chariots, not the scenery," he muttered. "Saw my father standing out on the pole urging his horses as they crashed through the shield-wall. It closed behind him like iron teeth." Iain sighed. "I had a thong and a handful of stones."

With Iain subdued, Tinker had been able to make time to the coast hoping to find a nice B&B with secure parking. Mr. Pockets would take a contract on his kneecaps if he got this latest penis-extension nicked. The main road was quiet, most sensible people being sat down to dinner, and at last Tinker could let the lunging brute take the bit in top gear. The Vee got to stretch its legs and the prospect of a butter-grilled 'smokie' haddock for breakfast in Arbroath was two miles closer with every minute. The old Lunan Bay side road was just coming up when Iain went manual.

"Stop!" bellowed the voice on Tinker's lips. Brake and clutch levers were pulled to the bars by an irresistible grip while engine and rubber screamed in protest—Iain never did take his motorcycle road test.

Tinker managed to regain control, all crossed-up in the road and thanking his stars for the absence of traffic. "Look, Iain," he exclaimed with some heat. "I do the riding here. Imagine me telling you how to fight."

"You were riding past my grave," muttered Iain, almost embarrassed.

That stopped Tinker. Other than to boast of its excessively heroic nature, Iain didn't dwell on the circumstances of his violent demise, but it had smelt of chthonic magic. Tinker's hand stole to the little stone Willendorf Venus pendant he always wore; she had gone warm and pliant against his chest, a sure sign of her approval. It was always best to please mum. *Magnus Mater* liked prehistoric monuments, especially ones with the Pictish women's symbols of comb and mirror—she also never forgot the little sacrifices of her champions. He sighed and engaged first gear; Lunan Bay it was.

A footpath to the headland proved motorbike accessible, at least to a necrophilic Pict with axe-hardened arms and the favour of a goddess in him. Tinker parked the mud splattered Vee in the eroded red sandstone ruins of an old castle commanding the bay. This would have to do for the night; at least he had his camping gear and it didn't look like rain. He could feel Iain was winding up for something and, like being stuck on a bad acid trip or a skittish bike, he'd just have to ride it out.

Evincing an uncharacteristic desire to purify himself, Iain virtually dragged Tinker down to a small river that wound through the dunes. Thankfully it was deserted as he undressed; predictably it was freezing. Then Iain persisted in forcing him to rummage around on the sandy bottom until he unearthed a bloody great lump of gneiss stone. There were smaller bits all over the place; but no, Iain wanted the big one.

"It has to go back where?" bellowed Tinker. The slab felt easy a hundred kilos and that was the only easy thing about it. Slippery with mud and algae, sharp-edged and awkward, it was all Tinker could do to drag the damn thing up on to the sandy bank.

Iain, as always, mocked his efforts. 'Hefted bigger axe-heads' was his version of encouragement. However there was no dissuading him, not even a break for a chilled Tinker to pull his boots on, let alone get dressed. You'd think the sun couldn't set without the task being accomplished, but Tinker knew ritual and tradition were everything at funerals.

Tinker squatted with the slab at his back. He jogged and worked out pretty regularly with weights, however there's a big difference between well-balanced iron and raw stone. Tinker got his hands under the rock, leaned it against his back, took a deep breath, and strained.

The Venus pendant throbbed on his chest, and then he felt a galvantic electric current shoot up through chilled feet and supercharge his muscles. Tinker jerked upright like an epileptic with the shock of it, and the stone came with him, its jagged surface biting like teeth into his bare back.

"Aye, a wee bit o' warp to start the softie," clucked Iain disapprovingly, and taunted Tinker into making a first step . . . "another, c'mon one more". The sand sucked at Tinker's feet, the heavy stone jolted, abrading his flesh, and sweat ran stinging into his eyes. At last the relief of firm grass sward, but then it tilted inexorably upwards and the real strain began.

Halfway up, Tinker fell to one knee, crying out as the jagged stone stamped its mark deeper with the impact. He could taste iron in each straining breath, and every snatched gasp tore at his bruised ribs. Iain was a pillar of support on this road to Calvary.

"Och and what's wrang? Any maid might bear the weight of a big man and smile the more for it," he goaded. "I mind fine I could haud on a branch and lift a pony wi' the grip o' my thighs."

Tinker bit his tongue for the motivation of pain, and strained to his feet again. The grass was still wet from the rain, his hands slippery with blood and the ever-present stone shards cutting his feet, yet he staggered on. There was more here than Iain's sadistic whims; other feet had imprinted the same sod with their travails, had strained under unconscionable burdens. All that stone didn't get there on its own, and if they could, he could. Most folk figure magic is getting yer kit off and prancing about chanting gibberish. The real shit hurts, costs, and no blood, sweat, or tears a sweeter sacrifice than your own. Like lifting weights; no pain, no gain. You stop feeling pain, you're dead.

Tinker stumbled again, near spent.

"Heave ho," whispered a woman's voice who was not a woman; just a trace of anxiety.

His vision wavered. He wept and drooled out baby noises. There was only the unforgiving weight versus his naked will. Phantoms seemed to toil alongside, urging him forward with their efforts. He was way past the pain barrier: this was do or die. Tinker was standing outside of himself, much further and he'd not be getting back in.

A moment's blackness, then he was sprawled on the ground throwing up, the sharp end of the stone jammed upright in the earth at his back. Tinker concentrated on breathing between the retches.

"That's where I died," said Iain quietly. "With a spear in my guts and a sword through the gizzard, not counting the arrows. I thought I had company enough."

"And fell alone defending the mother-stone ringed by their corpses," whispered the goddess. "Men have forgotten sacrifice."

I can't imagine why, thought Tinker, trying to focus his blurred vision as major endorphins kicked in. Now he was seeing mocking faces under winged helmets, intangible swords hacking as he lay like one dead. Then virtual flames surrounded him, his back frying against the burning stone. It seemed to expand into a towering monolith glowing red hot with indignities. Tinker felt as if his brain was boiling, about to burst from his skull—something had to give.

The dream stone exploded into meteoric fragments that ripped the Viking phantoms into shards. Then only blackness . . . and time.

Tinker struggled awake to cold, pain, and a woman's insistent voice.

"No, no more," he begged hoarsely.

"You should have told that to the barmaid last night," giggled the voice. A young woman in a jogging suit stood before him holding his boots and leathers. He realised he was shivering naked with a puddle of puke in front of him—definitely not the best first impression.

"Better get dressed," she urged. "I found these by the burn and followed your footprints. It's a wonder you're not dead of exposure, man."

Tinker strained to his feet, gasping in pain as his back unstuck from the stone.

"What happened?" she asked, real concern showing in her voice.

Tinker reached for his clothes. "I needed the exercise." The cuts on his back reopened as he struggled into his t-shirt and pants.

"You mean you carried that all the way up here?" She stared at him with a mixture of awe and disbelief. She looked more closely at the stone as if to convince herself it was real. "Hey," she exclaimed, "what's this?"

Tinker followed her gaze, then rubbed blood off the stone with his hand. He hadn't seen a relief carving on the stone before, yet there was one now, sharp as freshly-cut type. He'd been seeing pictoglyphs on the stones all yesterday and recognised the enigmatic 'sea elephant' design, but this one was subtly different. Sure it had those two peculiar spirals, more like wheels than legs, but he'd never seen a man on one before. Uh oh, now that backward reaching 'trunk' made sense with a rider's hands gripping it.

"Oh!" she gasped. "It's on your back too, all cut into it.'

"What!" Tinker pulled off the t-shirt. The 'elephant' and rider were there imprinted in blood. Hunting party or patch club: you perform a great feat of strength, will, and hardihood, then you receive your colours. Welcome to the elite, Pictish-style.

Nothing like mysterious heroes and spilt blood for a lady's . . . ah, sympathy, thought Tinker. A bloody great shiny bike didn't hurt either, truth to be told. He reached down and patted the five gallon fatbobs, all curved like . . . Tinker's attention snapped back to the road; too much fun makes you careless. He was beat, but Iain was happy as a clam and the little stone Venus curled against his chest like a contented puppy—he'd got points for this one. Returning the core of the mother stone as a marker to her fallen champion's deeds was very much in Pictish tradition. That's why dogs cock a leg to piss and men erect great stones—to mark their spot and show how high they have reached.

The big Vee was happy too; its hundred inches were eating up the tarmac at as many miles-per-hour and not even beginning to break a sweat. In a way it was like Iain, he could run all day and catch hares in the heather. Simple, utterly reliable, and too big for today. Mr. Pockets would soon get tired of the Vee's baulky lugging around town, and scare himself shitless every time he summoned the nerve to open it up. Tinker knew Pockets would be selling it for a less challenging pose, and muggins would be there with his wallet hanging out. The Vee was just so much like Iain, and Tinker a sucker for lost causes—men or machine.

He grimaced, and looked down at the 'skull-face' dash. Christ! Bastard was off the 120 mph clock again. Tinker couldn't turn his back on Iain for a second but he'd be twisting on the throttle or someone's throat. However, he was utterly loyal to his clan, and Tinker was very definitely clan now.

Tinker slowed the bike to a reluctant seventy, wincing as he sat up and cricked his aching shoulders straight. He felt blood trickle from the barely scabbed engraving; it wasn't something you'd get neatly stitched-up anymore than *stigmata* or Heidelberg sabre scars. When you ride with Picts, their colours don't come off with your leathers: those are just dead animal skins. Even outlaw club tattoos are pin pricks compared to stone-cut scarification and Tinker knew fine he'd be carrying a marker to the grave.

He laughed into the wind—come to think of it, he already had.

DEATH IN THE DAM

The Dutch sure know how to live, Tinker decided, tipping his chair back against the half-panelled wall.

A litre of fresh draught Heineken in one hand and a glowing cone-spliff in the other was proof positive. His latest ride, shining through the coffee house window on a street barred to cars, confirmed it.

One of the consolations for getting older is the bigger toys. One hundred cubic inches of V-twin was a tad overkill, especially in Amsterdam where pedal-power held sway, but out on the *autobahns* his Super Vee could crank it on with the big dogs. Maybe that accounted for its name—*Ubermensch.* All of Tinker's bikes had names, and personalities to match. Not that a loony biker just off the ferry fazed the locals one jot, used as they were to dope cafes and whores openly displaying their charms in Rosse Buurt storefront windows.

Tinker glanced at the clock, and smiled wistfully. Jan could be rolling in the door any minute now—apart from the fact that was twenty-five years ago and him serving life without parole. Tinker felt he had to re-visit the old rendezvous and sit at their table whenever he was passing through the 'dam. You leave parts of yourself in special places and they call you back to their shining moment, they beckon from your youth. How can we resist what made us?

Sentimentality is a middle-aged muse, but Tinker let it take him back to older, wilder days when the Rookies was just a pub and before the Leidseplein became a tourist trap. Tinker's first night in the 'dam all those years ago, he'd run into Jan right here—and finally come up against someone crazier than himself.

The hash-spiked spliff performed its magic, and he recalled the early seventies when they found out that the Rotterdam Harley dealer was lumbered with a bunch of ex-police K-models that nobody wanted. Jan talked the boss into a two-for-one deal, plus some desperately needed performance parts installed with a full service. They toured Europe, and riding hotted-up cop bikes with Dutch plates they pretty much got away with murder.

Tinker smiled as the memories had their little play and took another leisurely swallow on his Heine; funny how beer always tastes better close to the brewery. He recalled some of their epic beer-cellar brawls and high-speed pursuits, usually with him right behind Jan, who was always faster, tougher—and the one who started it.

Tinker sighed. Another, more thoughtful pull on the spliff and he watched smoke rise to dissipate itself on the nicotine-stained ceiling. Memories were going sour. Their parting of the ways wasn't really about the girl . . . what was her name? It was just that Jan was a runaway hell-bound train and Tinker had decided to get off at an earlier station.

Tinker sighed, the spliff went out. He left it in the ashtray alongside his helmet and gloves while he went to the can. Okay, he'd performed his little ritual; now it was piss, swill the last of the ale, then blast off to Tony's, his Indian dealer buddy in Lemmer.

Returning, Tinker was mildly irritated to see someone sitting at his table. It wasn't like the place was crowded and he had marked his spot. Some old guy all hunched over in a wheelchair. Maybe it's the crip's regular table now, Tinker figured, taking his seat. He reached for his beer and the big roach. "Okay if I smoke?" he asked, huffily polite.

"Don't care if you bursted into flames, Tinkerbell," whispered a voice from the past.

The roach fell from Tinker's fingers, and he stared at the stranger's face. "Jan?" Tinker gasped. Jan had been two years older than him; now it looked more like twenty, and none kind.

"Christ, it is you!" Tinker blurted out, quickly lowering his voice. "You're not on the lam, are you?" A big, foreign, hairy biker found smoking dope with a disguised, escaped . . . well, murderer, wasn't too swift even in easygoing Amsterdam.

Jan, or his ghost, peered at him from behind thick, tinted glasses. He didn't look to have any hair under the toque, or fat under his parchment skin, or long for this world.

"Yes, I . . . I, Jan Kramer." The familiar voice hacked with painful laughter. "I look in my rear-view mirror, and Tinkerbell is there no more."

Thank Christ, thought Tinker, remembering the rumours that had come his way after their split-up. Jan became a Dutch Emmett Grogan, a real Jack-the-Lad in full performance mode. Drugs, outlaw clubs, heavy shit going down. Still, Jan had been like a brother once, and that's a brother always. Goes for double when a brother's down this low.

"Jan, you crazy fucker," marvelled Tinker, clapping him on an emaciated shoulder to confirm his reality. "Forget our bygones, lemme buy my old riding buddy a beer 'n a hooter of hash."

A thin hand waved at the fresh-squeezed orange juice before him. "No alcohol, no drugs, definitely not the crazy fucking." A pale smile flitted across his ravaged face. "Compassionate release. They let me die on my own time to save themselves the trouble of burial."

Hard to lie with the truth staring you in the face. The truth was Jan looked like Rock Hudson's zombie. "Hey, Jan," Tinker jollied, knocking on the beer-ringed tabletop for luck like they used to. "Remember. Never say die."

Jan just looked at him from bone-tired eyes; just looked. A giggle of girls over by the pinball machines underscored the silence that fell between them.

"You were always too soft, Tinkerbell. How you say? Away with the fairies," Jan wheezed. "That was why you quit; too much of thinking, not enough the doing."

I could figure the writing on the wall, thought Tinker, but only said. "The fast life was your open road. I just couldn't keep up."

Jan's laughter was painful to hear, like an echo lost in his hollowed-out chest. "Not even on the same bikes or the same girls."

Tinker had to smile, it was true. Jan had such a big life force, events just gravitated around him: women, adventures, casualties. Jan never seemed to get hurt, and so self-possessed he could always charm his way out. It was scary to see him barely flickering in the ashes of a once-perfect body.

"Hey, Jan," Tinker cajoled. "It's never too late for hope."

His gaunt companion raised the juice in a mock toast. "But always too early for death, yes? Your timing though, it is just right."

Tinker didn't like the sound of that, gypsy riders aren't meant to be predictable. "In time for what, exactly?" he asked.

Jan smiled an off-centre grin. "What do you think? I hear you develop the second sight, a regular little Harry Potter, no?"

Tinker re-lit his spliff and looked casually round the bar, he didn't like going into full 'sight' in public. It looked too much like a seizure and people tended to stuff his wallet between his teeth, assuming they didn't run off with it.

The barman was explaining to a tourist that he couldn't sell him a whole ounce, much to the amusement of the local barflies. A rasta was putting the make on some Swedish blonde over in the corner. Tinker could just hear that old story—"Hey mon, yo not prejudiced or sumthin?" Over the other end, one of the teen gigglers had detached herself from the games and was heading towards their table, probably to bum a florin. Tinker tried to ignore her, but panhandlers always zeroed in on him.

"No, Jan," she said coming up behind them. "Tinker doesn't need his sight. I'm here."

The toke caught in Tinker's throat. He knew that voice, one you don't forget—it was from the grave. Jan pulled off his glasses with a shaking hand and stared hard at the teenybopper in her punk threads as she helped herself to a seat. That blanched Goth make-up wasn't, anymore than those kohl-rimmed eyes were a girl's. Girls are human. Jan nodded slowly—they'd met.

"Jeez . . . ack . . . Death." Tinker struggled to speak. "Do you have to sneak up like that?"

Jan found voice, and a trace of his old spirit. "Of course she does, even when she's expected," he croaked, "But I see you two have already met. I'd not thought you kept such dangerous company, Tinkerbell." He waved three thin fingers at the barman. "Jenevar, doubles."

Death put her pretty head on one side. She liked the brave ones, men wild to the bitter end. "Well, maybe for just one—while you boys talk over old times."

Last words, thought Tinker, stifling a groan. *I'm the wrong side of a bloody confessional here.*

The gins arrived. Tinker immediately shot his back, followed by a chaser of beer. Death emptied hers into Jan's orange juice with a lady-like prissiness and leaned back, looking speculatively around the room. Jan took a lingering sip of Jenevar and rolled it around in his mouth.

"First in fifteen years," he muttered, and took another. "Better I should have stuck to booze, it don't carry viruses." He pulled up the sleeve of his loose jacket; the old needle-scarred veins were white lines on the highway to hell. "Of course it could have been the 'boys' inside—we shared them too. Different world in there, Tinkerbell."

Tinker fiddled with the roach. Pricks in arm or arse were never part of his comfort zone. He'd heard rumours of bad stuff, but Jan had been like an older, wilder brother and Tinker had preferred his memories. Denial had come easier than sitting facing this picture of Dorian Gray—listening to it all spew out.

Death, on the other hand, never turned a jet-black hair. She'd heard it all in every language and convolution. Boring. Whatever.

"I can't complain, life was good till I turned it bad," Jan continued. "Just one regret." He looked at his hands holding the shooter of gin, pale translucent skin stretched over bone. "Remember Marlene?"

That was her name, Tinker thought. *Dirty Lilee; what a body.*

"She was the wild one, no? We even fought over her; kinkier the better for Lilee." Jan's eyes were hollower than his laugh. "Our last time, she thought it was just the 'rough scarfing'. But I'd found she was ratting me out to a business rival. I—we—had been using heavily and life wasn't worth much. It was the way she'd have wanted to go." He smiled thinly. "I can think of worse."

Tinker's chair clattered as he half-rose to his feet with clenched fists. "You strangled Marlene while you were screwing her?"

Jan looked up at him without emotion. "Just one more body they never found; I was not even charged." He motioned weakly for Tinker to sit down. "You were right to leave me. I'd only have damned you too."

"Hey, that stuff's no joke," cautioned Tinker. "I sort of got into magic over the years, and I've seen Hell. You're not gonna like it."

Jan smiled sadly. "But perhaps I have looked into it longer than you." He turned to Death, a black and white picture of teenage ennui sipping at her gin and orange. "Time for a last wish, yes?"

"Jan did buy you that drink," Tinker pointed out, knowing Death abhorred an undischarged debt to the quick. He'd decided he owed Jan one too, a last one for an old brother. "If it's in my power, let me grant the wish."

Tinker kicked the big, Chevy-based Vee twin into roaring life, then stepped back kicking himself. Jan insisted on getting from his wheel chair to the saddle unaided and just sat there, grinning like a skull and blipping the throttle.

"I give Lilee your regards, Tinkerbell," Jan said, and clasped him by the wrist in their old shake. The last time had been like this too. Jan off on a highway to hell with the bike and the girl.

Jan turned to Death. "So, come on baby, we ride to your place, no?"

Death hopped on, hitching up her leather mini. "I give the directions now, Jan." She liked big motorcycles; they put many fine young men her way. "Don't frown like that, Tinker, I won't let him wreck your baby. Ciao."

Away in a screech of rubber and scatter of bicycles down Korte Leidse Dwarsstraat. Tinker winced, hearing the poor engine howl and transmission clang at a speed-shift. Then he couldn't see them anymore, didn't need to. He knew the ending already. Tinker had just turned back to the coffee house when a distant, final scream of abused rubber ending in a loud splash, paused him in his tracks.

Tinker sighed, went inside, and got on the phone to Tony. "Hey, buddy, Tinker here . . . spot of bike bother . . . yeah, I know it's a long way . . . bring the truck with the power-winch and grapple . . ."

Tony eventually stopped laughing. Tinker hung up the phone and sat at a window table. He ordered a black coffee, and watched life go slowly by on pedals.

WHITE WHISPERS

Not everybody cries for help, many never even ask. Sometimes you just have to feel it inside. That's what friends are for.

Tinker scratched in his curly black beard and stared at the advert: '1948 Indian Scout—cheap for quick sale. Cash only.' He didn't recognise the post office box, but there were only racing Scouts made in '48 and no mistaking the particular example in that grainy photo.

The magazine slipped from his fingers as he felt the first tingle of prescience. Tinker might have lost touch with the bike scene and old riding mates the last few years, but he knew Bruce would never sell Pocahontas—something was very wrong.

Tinker's second sight took over his eyes, and they rolled back in his head as he went deeper. Fortunately he was sitting alone at his kitchen table; a reputation for epileptic seizures doesn't endear you to other riders. Controlling the vision was second nature now, bit like amateur photography or keeping an old bike in tune. Nice to have something to show for years as a virtual sorcerer's apprentice—and all the neglected friendships. He summoned the memory of Pocahontas from her photo, even in newsprint there's a little bit of soul captured.

Poke, as Bruce always called her, was one hot squaw and that photo hadn't done her fiery nature justice. Started as a model 648 factory racer; bench flowed, stroked, and ball-jobbed by Bruce into a wicked little scalp-huntress. They'd been broken and mended together; always came back faster. Tinker switched focus to Bruce; it wasn't hard, that flame-brain and his fire-engine red Indian were inseparable. Selling Poke would be like Bruce selling his soul—something very bad was going down.

Tinker concentrated, reaching past his vision of Bruce to the real thing. If some fool had stolen Poke, he'd have been doomed the minute that magazine hit the streets—unless Bruce was dead. Yet Bruce wasn't dead; Tinker had detected the pulse of his life force, but it was all over the place like static. He'd never liked strobe-lit discos; he sure didn't like these flashes of an angry boss, tearful wife, bike wrecks, fights. It was a life running out of control, out of time. Bruce must have been playing a game of snakes & ladders with his soul—and losing.

"Hello, is that you, Doris?" Tinker enquired in his Sunday-best voice.

"Who's asking? The woman's voice sounded tired, suspicious. She sure didn't sound like the Doris he remembered, yet it was Doris.

"It's me, Tinker. I was at your wedding." He hoped she didn't blame him—after all, he'd introduced her to Bruce.

The voice was cold, past pain. "That's over."

"Er . . . yeah, I heard, Doris." Tinker hastened on. "That's kinda why I'm calling outta the blue. I got this feeling Bruce is in dead trouble and . . . Well, I was his friend."

He heard the hard drag on her ciggie through the 'phone, the cough loud in his ear.

"He used to have plenty." She sounded like Marianne Faithful on a bad morning. "You're the gypsy, the one that could never settle."

Tinker seized on that. "Yeah, I fixed up old bikes for a living then. Never did get married, always too busy with other stuff."

Doris's laughter was a seal's bark across an ice flow. "I heard about your other stuff." There was silence, then, "Meet me at 'The Rose'." She hung up. She didn't have to say when; that voice meant now.

The Rose was an old, working man's pub. It used to have a rockers club room at the back with a small courtyard—perfect for bikes.

The back room was empty now, apart from some bag woman huddled over her drink, so Tinker went over to the fly-spotted window. He used to watch the bikes from here, watch the girls compare who had the biggest. *You couldn't miss Doris,* he reminisced. *What a cracker she was back then.*

"Not speaking are we, Tink?"

He nearly dropped his pint, that ruin in the shady corner was Doris! She'd pulled back the hood of her threadbare coat and was looking hard-eyed at him.

Tinker could barely meet her gaze, all that mane of wild black hair cut short as a dyke and shot with premature cobwebs of grey. She seemed shrunk inside her skin like a long forgotten party balloon. *No more parties left in that face,* he figured. Those weren't her teeth, and if a plastic surgeon had done that to her nose she'd be rich. Tinker assumed he could rule out rich.

The eyes were worst, almost no life left in them. Tinker had seen eyes in the supermarket fish freezer regard him with more feeling. The way she flinched at sudden movements as he grabbed a chair, Bruce must have all but knocked the daylight out of her.

"Sorry, Doris, my peepers ain't what they were," Tinker apologised unconvincingly and held out his hand.

She regarded it like he held a snake. "I know it's not your eyes, Tink. You always saw too much for your own good." She lit a ciggie, cupping the match. "Look close at me if you want to know about Bruce."

Under-lit by the flame, her features showed every care mark and scar. It was like she'd been sucked dry and Tinker wouldn't have been surprised to see tooth marks on her neck,

"Even if Bruce turned bastard I still gotta try." Tinker held out his hands in apology. "He was a mate."

Doris shrugged, and tapped the ash from her fag. "He'll use you up too—users and losers." She looked at him, almost pityingly. "How did you find out?"

"Saw Pocahontas for sale in a mag," Tinker explained. "You know what she meant to him—he must be completely desperate."

To his surprise, a tear made its way down her face, like sleet on stone. "Thank God," she breathed. "It's nearly over."

Her released emotion hit Tinker in a cold wave, he almost gasped. She'd never be able to breath free, not as long as B . . . "Hey! He's not dead yet, you gotta tell me where to find him."

He grabbed her hands. So thin, and the nails all chewed to jagged stubs. Doris had always been so particular about her hands. She tried to pull away, but there was little strength left. "C'mon, Doris, you're scaring me," Tinker snarled. "What kinda trouble is he in?"

Frail fingers twisted and dug the cigarette into the back of his hand. Tinker let go.

"Bruce isn't in trouble, it's in him." Doris hissed. "More than just the fucking white stuff and beating-up on people—it's like he's possessed, just pure evil." She jerked herself up and headed for the door. "You can forget quacks and shrinks; it would take a bloody magician to reach him."

Doris turned at the door, her voice bitter as alum. "You used to be queer for that shit, Tinker. Know a good 'un?"

Tinker went to the post office listed. It took little effort to project a glamourie of Bruce from memory; face-dancing can be ever so handy.

The clerk remembered him, was glad to see him looking so much better. He checked the address on file, quite unconscious of reading it aloud as he closed the box. Psychic projection was one of Tinker's easier subjects; his Irish gypsy side could sell blind pit-ponies to jockeys.

The address was a squat, and the vibes enough to see off any but the most determined eviction squad. Nothing grew in the front garden except broken glass and rust. It stank of cat piss and spoilt blood; but to the trained nose, there was a worse smell.

Tinker was enormously tempted to crunch the Indian Chief back into first gear and split; his silver skull 'n bones ring mocked him as he forced fingers to the ignition switch. Tinker blipped the wire-in-bars throttle to hear it roar, hit his horn twice, then killed the eighty-inch mill—their old 'let's ride' call.

Silence. Then he heard the whispers.

They were quiet as mice on snow-flake feet. He couldn't make out what they were saying. Yet they were there, lapping at the island of his consciousness like in-coming wavelets, icy little tongues.

The front door creaked open revealing a gaunt figure hunched over in the shadows.

"I see they're letting tinkies ride decent horses now." It was a voice from the past, like an old shellac record in poor shape. Bruce, alive, but barely.

Tinker had recently put together his 1939 bobber Chief and was breaking it in for a customer. With the baffles turned open it could wake the dead; well, nearly dead for sure. Bruce could never resist the flat bark of an Indian. Alas, never doesn't seem to last as long as it should, and Bruce didn't venture past the shadowed doorway. It didn't look like he could.

Tinker crunched through the debris and grabbed Bruce by the wrist in their old anarchist handclasp. He let go like he'd accidentally caught hold of a strange woman's tit. Bruce, who he'd seen bend handlebars straight with his massive, freckled forearms—now they were rail-thin. Tinker felt something else too: it had been like shaking hands with a fish, something come up from the bottom.

Bruce turned and shakily made his way back into the darkened front room. Poke sat in a clean spot in the middle of the filth pile Bruce obviously lived in. A shaft of light struggled through dusty curtains and caught the nickel plated chrome-moly frame and girder forks that carried her 'Big Base' racing engine. The tank art was too risque even for a B-17 nose cone. A very non Disney-like, and somewhat Betty Page, Indian maid posed the question 'Feeling Brave?' Tinker had known Poke to see off big-inch

Harleys, Triumphs, and even the odd unsuspecting Japper. Her second gear wound out forever and Bruce seldom shifted up to third under the ton.

Tinker thought he could hear the whispers clearer now he was inside: snatches of " . . . never ride it again . . . serves him right . . . think of the fun we could have . . . ." That last bit came through clear and persistent as a draught spot on a long, cold ride.

He tore his eyes from the temptation of her chrome-bright curves and looked hard at Bruce, now sunken in the ruins of a big, old-fashioned armchair. Second sight needs less illumination than a cave. Bruce's warrior namesake reputedly learned patience from studying a spider—he seemed more like the fly now.

Doris had looked kinda anemic, but Bruce could have been getting blood transfusions from Keith Richards. His soul lay very close-fitting under what little flesh he had left. Bruce was all but eaten away from within like some unfortunate caterpillar hosting a wasp's parasitic grub. He was just hunger and skin.

"Death already has his name," whispered that faint, cold voice probing his ear. "But you, you are strong." A woman's voice; yet not a woman.

Bruce sure looked spent, lost in the rat-gnawed armchair amidst mouldy take-out cartons and six pack rings. The spilt box of baking soda on the long coffee table was there to cook up crack, not abate the rotten odours. That sawn-off pump action wasn't for display purposes either.

Talk about meet me on the dark side of the spoon, thought Tinker. It wasn't just the chemical reek of crack-works, there was a thin, metallic taint discernable through the general decay. It smelled of sick mercury. It reminded Tinker of Hell. You don't forget anything about Hell.

"Bruce," he said urgently, reaching over, virtually kneeling in the garbage. "How long you been this fucked-up, buddy?" He forced himself to look deeper at Bruce. Life sputtered but faintly behind those dead, Kurtz-cursed eyes.

Bruce struggled, but seemed unable to talk. He painfully extended three fingers. Three years, thought Tinker. Renewal time for spells, covenants, and simple possession.

"Heed not a junky's lies," came the whisperer again, now clear as a tiny bell and so close it brushed his ear. "It's too late for him."

Tinker recognised truth even when insinuating from the tongue of a demon, but Bruce wasn't dead yet. Besides, it's only how you die that matters.

"So, you need cash bad enough to sell Poke?" Tinker asked. "Didn't you think I'd help a mate?"

Bruce seemed to be scratching weakly in his matted red hair, but Tinker still remembered their road code. Wooden hulled wind-riders used coded flags; long-distance bikers had their own signs in hostile environments, and Bruce was patting his head—watch out, trouble about. Fingers strayed to his ear lobe—someone listening. Tinker got it, his thumb moved imperceptibly upwards—right.

"Knew you'd help. No other way to reach you." Bruce managed a weak smile, but with fewer teeth than Tinker recalled.

"Fuckin' 'ell, man," cried Tinker, feeling the tears mount in his eyes. "How did you get like this?"

Another faint twinkle, then a tortured whisper forced itself out through clenched teeth. "Devil made me do it." Bruce's smile twisted in a spasm, Tinker could almost see the coke bugs digging in under his skin. " . . . just joking, Tink," Bruce gasped, but two fingers stuck out—forked tongue, horns.

So that was it, demon for sure. Hard drugs are for softies and it would have taken more than just powdered pleasure to seduce a tough nut like Bruce. *Have to be a female demon too. He was always the sucker for a pretty face,* reasoned Tinker, *and now it'll be looking for a fresh ride.*

He walked over to Poke; Bruce had cut holes in the floor and wrapped a chain around the joists to secure the bike. Tinker reached into his jacket and tossed a manila envelope on to Bruce's lap. "Sign those papers and gimme the keys." He took out a much thicker envelope. "Got five thousand quid there, used notes."

Bruce hurriedly scrawled his name as directed, passing the documents over with his key ring in exchange for the money. He tore the envelope open with trembling fingers. Tinker unlocked the heavy chain, then walked back over to where Bruce crouched counting the cash.

"It's all there. Trust me," Tinker assured him, looking over Bruce's shoulder. Quickly he wrapped a turn of chain around Bruce and the heavy chair, slamming the lock shut. He kicked the shotgun away before Bruce could drop the cash and reach for it.

Bruce screamed and strained against his fetters, but they were iron and that big armchair was near twice his present weight.

"Money can't mend what you got, Bruce," Tinker said quietly. "Just prolong the agony. It's kill or cure time."

"Even you, Tink," Bruce raved. "You're all out to get me. I should have listened."

Tinker shook his head sadly, retrieving the cash and pump action from where they'd fallen. "You've listened too long, buddy," he said quietly. "Now I'm doing the talking, and it ain't to the organ-grinder's monkey."

He straight-armed the coffee table clear of crap, setting it lengthways so that it pointed at Bruce. Tinker moved a rickety chair up to the far end of the table and leant the gun against it. Next he pulled a baggie from his jacket pocket and poured a long, thick line of finely chopped crystal from Bruce to himself.

"You trying to torture me, huh?" Bruce whispered, sweat beading on his forehead. "Do you think I'll talk?"

No, Mr. Bond, I think you shall die, occurred to Tinker, but he took a none-too-clean hanky from his pocket, balled it up, and reached over to stuff it into Bruce's mouth. He winced as he felt a couple of teeth give.

"I said I wasn't talking to you." Tinker pulled out his belt knife and toyed with the powder, chopping it finer, straightening out the line. "You know, this here's top quality marching powder," he said absently. "Got it off a grateful eye doctor who'd seen far too much for his own good. Pure pharmaceutical devil's dandruff. Now, that reminds me of a story. You know how I never could resist a captive audience."

Tinker settled back in his chair. "You see, there was the king of Cork what became possessed by gluttony, sure he's eating the land bare to the bedrock. So they ups and gets in this holy man to cast out the royal demon. And doesn't he chain the king to a pillar, like yourself now, and start spinning this interminable story. It's all about oceans of cream and an island full of roast pigs, and all the time he's stuffing himself on the best grub and sending out for more." Tinker paused, stuck the tip of his blade into the bag, and conveyed it to his nose—spilling half the blow into his beard. He sniffed and sneezed, blowing most of it back out.

"Godfrey Daniels," Tinker cursed, scattering more from the baggie on to his leather riding pants. "Excellent toot, untouched by human foot—poetry, eh?" He stuck the knife into the table edge to keep it handy, and took a big pinch from the now near-empty bag. Tinker's black-leathered lap acquired another dusting of snow and Bruce's eyes bulged with drug-hunger at the profligacy.

"Now, where was I?" Tinker rubbed his nose like he was suspecting frostbite. "Oh yeah. So the poor king, he's gasping for a haunch of wild boar with crackling and a horn of mead to wash it down. But, to tell the truth, most of all he's gasping seeing as the demon's fed up waiting for dinner and is rising in his gorge."

Tinker was talking faster now, caught up in the tale and reverting to Irish gypsy roots. Despite his efforts, some of the coke had made it in and he wasn't used to hard drugs.

"So, out of the very mouth of the king, pops a demon's head. Not every day you get to see that, though I've often wondered about Thatcher," he continued, his hands acting out the drama. "So the saint, fine man that he is, grips Mr. Demon with the fire tongs and traps him under a bloody great iron cauldron."

Bruce was all but passing-out from sheer need. Tinker had to wing it. "For an encore, he shags the king's daughter and everybody lives happily ever after—except a poor starving demon. The End."

"I suppose you think that's funny," hissed a decidedly unamused voice right in his ear—it sounded very nasal now.

"Suppose I thought it might get your attention," said Tinker. "See, I don't deal with flunkies."

Bruce had sparked out, his eyes all white, and a presence was oozing from his sinuses like blood-laced ectoplasm. The shape floated in a malevolent cloud over his wasted face, a jellyfish feeding on a drowned man. It formed into an ethereal mask, the lips rippled.

"Don't you mean junkies, poor Adam-son?"

Tinker just hoped he could handle this. They say the smarter demons take their faces from your heart. This one had taken Jean's—easy with her dead these many years, hard with Tinker's love for his bonnie Jean still beating. *See you, Jimmy.*

"I mean I want to know who I'm dealing with," Tinker stated firmly.

Jean's face, if you'd starved her of food and light, smiled unpleasantly. "Only an amateur would think names were for the asking." The whisper was getting stronger, more confident. "But I have your name, Mr. Tinkerman."

"Nickname is no name," said Tinker, more evenly than he felt. "Only a mother has the true naming." He took another baggie from a pocket and poured the entire contents out at his end of the line. "And anyhow, I have your mother's name, you little alkaloid skim-off."

A visible shudder passed through the gel-like mask.

"Does dear old Erythroxylaceae know you're out riding men?" Tinker pressed his point. "I seem to recall her charter from the Green Queen was to help man survive in high, hard places. Seems to me you're doing it ass-backwards, and you must know that can reverse a spell."

The jelly-face quivered with rage and it grew, acquiring shoulders and an anorexic female torso. "My mother was no better than vegetative. Man was my father, he raised and refined me. Your meddlers alchemised your own demon—I have the claim of blood."

Tinker scratched in his bushy black beard, scattering surplus powder. "Hmm, sounds like we got a Mexican stand-off here." He reached absently for the shotgun. "Guess we'll have to have another Celtic history lesson; help pass the time and all."

The demon groaned out loud, but she couldn't reach this tormentor without leaving the host, and Bruce was her tether goat.

"Viscount John Graham of Claverhouse," announced Tinker. "Bonnie Dundee to his many friends, Bluddy Clavers to their enemies. He led the Jacobite charge at the battle of Killiecrankie, you know."

"I assume they lost," sighed the demon, anticipating a maudlin Celtic lament.

"Naw, the redcoats ran away, as usual," said Tinker. "Clavers never lost a battle, nor did Bonnie Prince Charlie till Culloden and even then only through listening to an Irishman's advice."

"So," grumbled the demon irritably, the Scottish tales were almost worse than the Irish, "what's your point?"

"Ah," replied Tinker, fiddling with his large silver skull ring. "You see, Clavers seemed to possess a charmed life, so everyone figured he had to be in league with a demon."

The ectoplasmic body stopped reaching for him, and grew wary.

"Anyhow, cut a long story short, a canny lowland marksman plucked the silver button from off his coat—just like this." Tinker pulled off his ring and demonstrated by stuffing it down the shotgun barrel.

Suddenly, he pointed it at the demon's head. "Bang. Poor old Clavers, struck down in the very moment of his triumph. Nasty stuff when it comes hot and fast, is pure silver. Works just like a ley-line, instant connection. Moon metal sure got the earth mother's power humming through it, and her so close to the Green Queen too."

He held the gun rock steady at point blank range. "Say, you never did tell me what yer mum thought about all this sort of malarkey; want I should plug you in to her?"

The demon wavered, looking from the inviting line of coke to his shotgun. "Perhaps it would be better if I found other accommodations."

It was as if a veil was being pulled from Bruce's mouth and nose, a veil too short to reach the glittering line without parting. Bruce gagged, his eyes flickered open then squeezed tight shut again at the sight. But, in that moment, he was Bruce again.

"That's right," encouraged Tinker as the form coalesced and bent over the table. "Follow the white line all the way." She was like the Japanese print Magic John had showed him once, a snow fox-maiden. Seductive as all evil, and so delicate you wanted to break it, you wanted . . . He pinched his nose very hard, and concentrated.

The demon oozed forward, snuffling at the powder with greedy intensity. Tinker hurried over and fumbled the padlock open while she was caught by her own device, quickly unwrapping the chain from a dazed Bruce. "Hope you can still ride," he whispered urgently, tearing out the gag. "The shit's about to hit the fan big-time."

Tinker dragged him bodily over to Poke and got a foot on the kicker pedal. The demon was growing in strength, fed by the line, and it had almost reached the heap at the end.

Brrammm! The open duals brayed a long-silent indignation, and the demon made a sudden pounce for the nose-candy mountain before the blast could hit it.

Tinker threw Bruce into the saddle. "Boot it," he yelled in his ear. "That pile's smack, another demon's territory."

An instant blizzard exploded from off the table like a shock wave struck between opposite electrodes. The exhaust's roar was lost in a terrible scream of indignation—with an off-key echo. As if in a crazy giant snowflake ball of energy, two demons were violently intertwined, all powdered over and neither looking very happy about it. Someone had definitely got up someone else's nose.

Tinker threw open the front door and flung himself behind Bruce as he tore out on the bike. "Didn't know . . . which drug had you," he gasped, trying to keep them upright. "Just as well . . . they're in competition for souls."

Bruce somehow managed to brake at the kerb without falling over. Leaping off, Tinker fired up his Chief almost, but not quite, drowning out the unbelievable howls emanating from inside the house. Sounded like a wildcat raping a racoon.

"You sure you're okay to ride?" Tinker said anxiously; in the direct sunlight he could see Bruce was fast running out of road.

"I'll . . . manage," Bruce husked, his hand shaking as it caressed the tank art. "Worse ways to go, eh, sword in hand?"

He snicked into first, and turned to Tinker. "Thanks, mate, I just don't know how to . . ." Words didn't come, just a shadow of that old teasing smile as he popped the clutch and screamed off down the road.

"You sneaky bastard!" Tinker shouted—cramming on the throttle in hot pursuit of a funeral.

—

BUYER BEWARE

Up before dawn, couldn't sleep, excited as a kid promised the circus.

Tinker pulled on clean socks and considered his T-shirt drawer,. Hmm? 'God Made Harleys to Keep Faggots off Indians'; perhaps a slightly lower profile might be recommended. There, *la fee verte* herself, on a reproduction of a *fin de sicle* Pontarlier absinthe label. Nobody could object to the Green Fairy—certainly not at Underhill's faery faire.

Many the way to the Fey. For himself, Tinker preferred old-fashioned iron pony. Pocahontas counted as family, or close as a stroker Scout you share a birthday with gets—and you can get pretty up-close and personal during high-speed pursuit. She had belonged to an old friend who died fast and demon-free in her arms.

Now Poke waited his pleasure below: fueled, fettled, and freighted with trade goods—primarily electronic tat picked up for dick off barrow boys and boot sale stalls. Man's modern 'magics' were silicon's version of glass beads for natives of the hollow hills.

Tinker took particular care over his toilet, hair carefully braided and beard combed. He'd showered last night after sorting out Poke and polishing his leathers, so just a quick wake-up splash. No brekkie, an empty stomach and clear skin radiate purity of purpose. Likewise care in attire; it advertises the gentleman, as does his steed. Best part of magic is a good show.

Couple of choked priming kicks, magneto on, fire in the hole. Tinker set the house-warding spell while Poke warmed her fifty-weight. Yesterday's wash and wax polish showed his vain little red racer to advantage as she perked in the rose-tinted dawn. You couldn't like bikes and not want to give her one.

Down the road and out of town, far from the tamed land of fields and up into the lonely old hills where flathead torque comes to play. Dawn hadn't dispelled the lingering high-moor mists yet; fortunately Tinker knew the way of the Fair Ones with his eyes shut—so he did.

Dropping to second, Tinker took a sharp downhill left that might not have been there if he'd peeked. He slowed as the gradient fell off and took another the same way. Turn again, a twist sinestral deeper into darkness. Then down to first for the tight last left that complete his widdershins spiral. Coast to a stop, peepers open again—Tarrah! Underhill, a.k.a. Fairyland.

The whole great common sat quilted with a rainbow of tents: yurts, marquees, tepees, stalls, you name it. The bustling clientele, from every dimension and belief system, added to the mix making variety the spice of life for market-faire. A calliope, tootling lustily, drowned the hawking cries of vendors, while a faint aroma of fresh-baked pies and malty waft from the brew tent competed to weaken his abstemious resolve. Coursing zephyrs teased through Tinker's beard then rushed up to fill the high pavilion banners, ensuring that he didn't notice the auroch dung till he dismounted and stepped in it. Goblin Market or Dire-Faire to doubters, Tinker wouldn't miss one for the world—well, bits like Kirby and Easterhouse anyway.

Tinker unbuckled the throw-over saddlebags, slinging them across his shoulder. No need for weapons here, the Fey deal most severe with those as break the market truce. Cutpurses who valued fingers kept them safe in their own pockets today. Everything else fair game in the match of wits and desire twixt seller and buyer. Haggling, for a gypsy, of course constituted half the fun.

Two cashiered nightmares were peddling alleged dream sand from a shabby booth on the periphery. Avoiding their crude blandishments, Tinker entered the great circle of tents encompassing Underhill common.

A quick detour to a favourite stall digging out spare packs of batteries and a gratis solar charger for Berz, the proprietor. Tinker had traded a cheap digital camera to him last time for a see-all monocle, Berz hadn't recogised its fine chain as mythral. Always pays to keep good customers sweet.

One thing led to another, and Tinker ended up trading a few more cameras for a recently whelped gorphon. It looked up at its new master from the palm of his hand, in form a tiny Staffordshire bull terrier wagging its brindled tail uncertainly. Gorphons will sit quiet in your pocket all day, yet leap out full-sized at a word and take on a tiger. Full-size for a pup would be about pit pony, and a seriously cross gorphon will give even a were-beast pause. All gorphons need a master and will take the form most likely to attract one that smells right. As a beardless teen Tinker had befriended a punchy English bull terrier, thrown out like him on the street. His name was Bonzo, and it took death to separate them: sadly, old dogs age quicker than lost boys.

Tinker smiled, plucked a small silver bodkin from his lapel, and jabbed it into the ball of his thumb. He held out the welling ruby droplet for the gorphon to lick.

"Henceforth you are Bonzo, and I'm Tinker, your new master." He stroked its back and tickled behind the ears. "You will safe-guard this blood as your own and be litter-mate to me and mine."

Now the tail became a blur. Not possessing a descended larynx, Gorphons can't articulate, but hear and sense very well indeed. Bit of effort and you can teach 'em to read and write.

"First job, Bonzo," Tinker continued, pointing out Poke. "Guard my bike, the red one over there."

Bonzo shot off, legs pumping like pistons. Presently Tinker saw a small shape proudly sitting up on his saddle. First deal of the day, and a true one.

Some well-remembered stalls, some new. A wave to the 'Living Tattoos' needle-fingered maestro, finishing a Silkie paint that shape-shifted from seal to man as you viewed it. A solar-powered calculator got gifted to the money changer's booth. The poor pencil-neck sorely needed digital assistance with the vast range of currency exchange calculations when barter failed. Extra special rates for Tinker from now on, eh!

He skirted the Punch and Judy stand, caught one recently and it had been a bit below the belt. Live music, however, lured him over to a small stage. A bunting-wrapped cart, in point of fact. The tired minstrel, sweating in motley, caught Tinker's fingers unconsciously copying his chords. He finished the song, and his lute-backed hurdygurdy fell silent.

"I do believe a volunteer from the audience will entertain us while I pass the hat." The player jumped off the stage, thrusting the instrument into Tinker's surprised hands. "It's guitar strung, just keep turning the handle," he whispered out the side of his stage smile. "Give you some of the take if you hold them while I collect."

The Irish in Tinker felt little loath to play a warmed-up audience. He mounted the cart and tried a few exploratory chords. It felt like playing one-handed without the finesse of right-hand finger picking, just that insistent, resin-wheeled drone. He needed a dirge, one with long roots and sharp hooks . . . sure now, 'Maria Martin' would do fine. Her murder in the red barn acquired many variants over hundreds of years and thousands of street corners.

"I said that I would marry her, upon a certain day.

Instead of which I was resolved, to take her life away . . ."

Ah yes, the eternal tale of an innocent girl betrayed by her false lover. Female, to his guess, members of the audience listened, and perhaps put a little extra into the fool's cap.

"Now all things being silent, her spirit could not rest.

She appeared before her mother, who suckled her at the breast . . ."

Listeners nodded, well they knew of unquiet dead. However, justice swift and severe brings penitence and rests a ghost.

"So come all you thoughtless young men, this warning take by me.

For murder of that young maid, to be hanged upon the tree."

The hat jingled as the entertainer climbed back on his cart. "Well played, friend," he complimented, holding out the takings. "Your pick as promised."

Tinker regarded the contents: sundry obscure narcotics, a glitter of semi-precious stones, tooth with a gold filling, a couple of silver buttons . . . no, tiny pre-war thru'penny bits. He scooped them in memory of his mum's Christmas dumpling, where they'd hide, tight-wrapped in twists of grease-proof paper, from his eager spoon. Besides, these beauties were mint-fresh, unlike the worn, wafer-thin ones he remembered. Worth quite a bit this perfect to a numismatist, soft silver and high circulation tends to make for a short life. As he waved farewell, Tinker made a mental note to pack his Stella next time. Rattle and hum the marks with some twelve-string 'claw-hammer' picking . . . oh, and a large hat.

A hungry rumble from below served notice on Tinker that his nose had led willing feet to Simon's pie stand, situated convenient to the 'Marquee of Ales'.

"Down boy," he muttered, determined to make at least one circuit before succumbing to pleasures of the flesh. That included 'Inanna's Sacred Strippers' next door, whose catwalk currently trembled to the terpsichory of Uzuma. Short and zaftig, Uzuma had been the Japanese Goddess of Merriment before they got too serious. Tub or no, she invented striptease and meat on the bone always appeals at a primitive level. Fat women make milk, their babies survive. The steatopygic Willendorf Venus pendant around Tinker's neck jiggled to the music, proving his point.

Wrenching away from such corporeal temptations, Tinker continued his counter-clockwise peregrinations. A hurry past the 'Bookworm Browsery' lest he be lured by another demon-ridden volume. A pause at 'Agreeable Reflections', caught by his framed image. Lustrous jet-black locks, all silver banished as were the road-wrinkles and roughness from his features. The reflection smiled invitingly, revealing teeth white and perfect as toilet tiles. *Christ! I look like a poof,* thought Tinker. Not that he had anything against the vice versa; company he kept, who scratched which itch had long ceased to matter.

Hullo! Who put the lights out? Tinker looked up expecting to see a cloud over the sun, then realized he had strayed beneath the shade of Underhill's great tree. A few years back he'd camped between the massive roots of Santa Barbara's football field-sized fig tree when riding the Pacific Rim - ah, simpler days. Snapping out of the memory, Tinker noticed lurkers in the umber darkness. Feral eyes weighed him from the tree's shadowed convolutions, and he didn't need to look far for the reason. A stand of that damnable goblin fruit had been set up between two main roots. Now he caught the sickly smell of black lotus and the compelling rot of forbidden growths. Goblins are like those Ferengi on the telly, nothing too dirty for profit. Small wonder the place resembled a bleeding Keith Richards look-alike convention.

One had the nerve, or desperation, to approach him. Female, human, young once but now more like Marianne Faithfull in her 'shag-for-skag' Soho days.

"Please, can you help me," she begged, trembling in an agony of trepidation and need. "I simply have to get away from this place."

Trendy little rich witch, Tinker figured. Magic had been quite the in-thing a couple of years back: still picking up the fucking pieces.

"You're human, a biker," she pleaded, dirty broken nails clawing at his leather sleeve now. "I used to have a Sportster once. I'd give absolutely anything for a ride out of here."

Panhandlers and damsels in distress were iron filings to Tinker's magnetic personality. Some kind of secret sucker sign he must carry around. Before he could set her straight, a goblin inserted himself between them.

"Regrettably, honoured sir," he began, rubbing unpleasantly long fingers like Uriah Heep. "The lady may not depart without her slate being cleared."

Tinker sighed, but playing the rube, opened his saddlebags. He pulled out a pen and lit up its selection of multi-coloured lights; for writing in the dark, cavity search, whatever.

The goblin's big yellow eyes lit up too. "Very pretty," he murmured, "very unique." Business quickly reasserted itself. "Yet for the lady's account it would require more than just one."

A brace of shake-down artists? Tinker mused, *or just a fucked-up girl in the hole to this drug pimp? Verily, a judgment for Solomon.*

"Tell you what, me old hobgob," he said affably. "I'm feeling peckish. Before we get to dickering, how about I swap this pen for a large basket of your finest produce?" The goblin hopped to it; not only such a deal, but fresh meat to bleed.

Carrying his newly traded spoils over to the shadow's edge, Tinker placed it down, then stepped out into the light. The girl had followed the big basket, devouring it with her eyes. The goblin followed her, a little less sure now.

"Here's the way it is, luv," Tinker stated bluntly. "Freedom or death: mine to offer, yours to take."

Her mouth started working, but only salivations came out.

"But that's not fair," she gasped, wrestling with the jones.

"Fair is entertainment for kids," growled Tinker. "This here's the market place and you've made yourself a commodity."

"I . . . I can't choose." Tears fell to beat rain and she shook like she was coming apart.

"You have to. Every moment, each waking day, for years—always you'll face this choice." Tinker laughed mirthlessly. "Hey, you chose to become an addict, you've chosen to remain one, so now you can choose not to."

He could have saved the lecture. She grabbed the basket and sprinted off into the dark shelter of the roots, clutching it tightly to her bosom. The goblin shrugged, one business man to another, nothing personal. She'd be back.

Tinker walked thoughtfully away. He had the distinct impression he'd just been conned in to standing that junky a hamper. Still, as any feminist will tell you, freedom of choice never comes free.

On past stalls full of fabulous, but unneeded, items till he came to 'Master Thyme's' secluded booth. Rich old men and women entered, younger and poorer they emerged; all very discreet, like the Monty Python wig department sketch. Hmmm! technically off-limits to Death, courtesy of an undischarged debt, Tinker aged nevertheless. Neither diet nor exercise can much delay the relentless rusts of oxidation. Magic, fortunately, can do almost anything and specializes in the impossible—at a price.

The 'Shooting Gallery' caught Tinker's ear before his eyes registered. Full choice of weapons, kill a proxy of your most hated enemy in the worst possible way. His thoughts of settling a few old scores evaporated before the spectacle of a middle-aged man wearing heavy knuckledusters. He was single-mindedly pounding a naked, obese woman, presumably his wife, into screaming mince.

Saddlebags emptied of solid-state trinkets and filled with desirable items: ounce of under-the-counter Everisle snout for Magic John—out smoke the burning bush that 'baccy would, quart of Kraken oil for Poke—stay cold as a deep sea trench and quite frictionless, and a freshly unwrapped mummy bone for lucky Bonzo. Basic ingredients too had been crossed off his shopping list: a baby's caul, phoenix feathers, mermaid scales, vial of unicorn blood—and then, all of a sudden, he'd done the Dire-Faire circuit. It occurred to Tinker that several libations were now in order.

Bonzo gnawed happily on a pharaoh's femur, and Poke leant outside digesting a generous shot of extra-virgin Kraken oil. Tinker sat at a nearby trestle table and brushed pie flakes from a beard purged of silver turnings. He felt, and to all appearance had become, ten years younger—and only for an iPod-clone packed full of early Negro blues. Nothing like spontaneous expressions of human misery to cheer up the Fey and Unseelie.

His pie and pint cost Tinker a LED Catherine wheel-effect hand fan. He'd grumbled at the price till his first, thirsty swallows failed to lower the level. Everale smuggled in from Everisle, the land of all things eternal—might as well be Thor trying to drain the sea. Imprinted by Scottish poverty to leave nothing to waste in dish or cup, Tinker swilled his hairy face off.

At the facilities, actually a half-screened trench out back where one stood, squatted or lifted leg as anatomy and need dictated. Tinker fought down his gorge at some of the offerings in the makeshift cludgie and was hastily zipping up when Bars appeared at his side.

"Hiya, Bars ol' buddy," slurred Tinker, everybody's friend on a surfeit of Everale. Bars, proprietor of Underhill's 'Greene Queen' hostelry and this most likely his beer tent too. "Didn't know you ever needed to . . ."

A smile twisted the burn tissue that comprised Bars' face. "Just because I'm not strictly speaking alive doesn't mean I'm a ghost, thank you," he grumbled, candle-stub fingers fumbling with the fly of his breeches. "The reanimated still have bodily functions to attend to."

Tinker couldn't help but peek, and immediately wished he hadn't. Being trapped in the cockpit of a burning Hurricane had done nothing for Bars' joystick.

"Thing is," said Bars, suddenly serious, "there's been a complaint."

With a shock, Tinker recognised the ceremonial chain of office around Bars' neck. "You're this year's Mayor of the Faire." Tinker gaped. "This is official business."

Bars smiled briefly, revealing heat-discoloured teeth beneath his flaming eponymous handlebar moustache. "A particularly nasty little goblin buttonholed me and said one of his regular customers sold off a big basket of his finest wares, paid up her tab, then scarpered. Claimed it was all your fault."

Tinker guffawed and slapped his leather-clad thighs. "Wow! She actually did it. Way to go, gal." He sobered up somewhat; after all, an official complaint could make him *persona non grata*. "Look here, Bars, Scout's honour. I bought that basket fair and square from the 'orrible 'obgob. Then I sorta let her take it, and walked away."

Bars rebuttoned laboriously and smoothed down his person. "That's pretty much what I assumed. You were always the softie, but never thief or cheat." Dress adjusted to his satisfaction, Bars regarded Tinker poker-faced—no stretch for scar tissue.

"I enquired whether his minders had witnessed this version of the facts, and he was quick to assure me they'd swear to it." He pulled a large silk handkerchief from his waistcoat pocket and polished the mayoral chain thoughtfully. "Told him they'd all have to come away with me to sign depositions." He coughed and replaced the kerchief. "We'd attracted quite a crowd, a rather desperate-looking bunch actually, but all nods and smiles now. Well, in short, he decided it might be wisest to let the matter drop—can't imagine why."

Tinker could. It would be like Afghan Poppy Day and Summer of Sixty-Seven once all that narco-fruit got left unattended. Poor old 'Crumpleforeskin' would be lucky if he returned and they'd left even the stand.

"Good old Bars." Tinker was still chuckling as he heaved a leg over Poke. On impulse he let Bonzo out of his pocket, "Wanna ride up front?" Frantic tail-waggings, and the tiny terrier hopped up to the bars, bracing himself on the Indian-face horn with his forepaws. Maybe gorphons can't speak, but his eager bark was a hound's for the chase.

Down on the kicker, blip the throttle to impress punters . . . then a shadow detached itself from the deep shade under an awning. *Damn, that bird again*! She had the shakes, yet her mouth set in determination.

"G . . . give a girl a ride?" she asked, sticking out a thumb that wouldn't keep still.

He sighed, and considered. She looked like hell on the half-shell, but her will shone through the dross. There's this glow about the reborn, a kind of magic. Hope, maybe—hard to come by these days.

"I meant it when I told you I'd do anything for a ride out of here," she reminded, sensing his weakening resistance.

Tinker turned the Edison-Splitdorf mag to full retard, but the motor still ran a tad fast. Hmmm, had to be that Kraken juice, uncanny absence of the usual rattles and whirrs too.

"What you mean is you're willing to trade your body for a return to Realityville." He fiddled with the bored-out Linkert until the urgent purr became a slow, steady pulse.

She nodded silently, urgently, a dash of colour to her wan cheeks suggesting this might be the first time she'd been desperate enough to whore her person.

Another big sigh, and Tinker reached back to unlimber the passenger pegs. Only one thing certain about the Dire-Faire, you never knew what you'd be coming home with.

BOODGIE WOODGIE

"If Irene turns her back on me, gonna take morphine and die".

Oops, thought Tinker, *should have stuck to the Lonnie Donnegan lyrics*. Still, it was Leadbelly's song, and him a hard-as-nails field niggra as could pick a bale of cotton then play barrel house or sukey jumps all night fueled by corn mash and cocaine.

The twelve-string jangle and hum rang in amplification off the marble art deco façade of the cinema as Tinker busked the afternoon queue. Switching to a lighter Al Stewart number, he regaled them with:

"It's well I do remember, the first time I put to sea.

It was on the old 'Calcutta' in eighteen fifty-three . . ."

Meanwhile Bonzo, Tinker's gorphon pup, waddled along the line of listeners with an old American half-helmet clamped in the alligator-like jaws of a brindle Staffordshire bull terrier. Piggy little eyes twinkled and his tail went like a metronome as spare change was tossed in. Like old Nipper cocking an ear to the phonograph horn, Bonzo enjoyed his master's voice.

In truth it wasn't a bad one, and as a street-teen Tinker had sung for his supper many the night. Not that he needed the dosh now, but it kept him in practice and the memory of harder times alive. He blamed his Irish gypsy dad who'd burst into song at the drop of a hat, or the level of his Guinness; for sure his good Scots mum would've died before performing in front of a crowd. Yet Tinker had the magic of music and conjurer's fingers for tickling paired steel strings with a full set of finger picks.

Getting into the sentimental swell of 'Old Admirals', Tinker failed to notice a spot of bother develop. Half-a-dozen loitering yobbos, tired of annoying folk in the line-up, had now turned on Bonzo.

"Stoopid little runt," snarled one hoodie, all boots and mouth. "Not like a proper dog."

Bonzo set down the well-filled helmet and put his head on one side; quite comical, but actually more like a shark about to strike. Would these scheme-born dropouts believe gorphons are creatures of magic? No, they didn't believe in nuffin' and not a shred of magic in their Orc-like lives.

One less wed-to-life skin made the mistake of trying to grab the takings. His psychic pulse brought Tinker's head snapping round before the screams even got started. Now, you don't use an antique Stella as a club, it gets laid gently aside in its case—then you wade into the scrum. Unfortunately, when you own a gorphon, you tend to miss most of the fun.

The punks as could still walk, ran. The other two mainly bled and made inarticulate pleading noises. Bonzo bounded over proudly, helmet and contents retrieved intact.

"Err . . . good dog," mumbled Tinker, rapidly pocketing the take before donning his vintage 'Masters' lid. He hustled the pup over to where Pocahontas, his Indian Scout bar-hopper sat parked, quickly zipping the guitar into its case cum backpack. Real blood tends to put off the punters no matter who started it, and Bonzo coughing up bits didn't help.

Right, time to split. Opposite side of the bike from the queue, Bonzo shrank down to a convenient traveling size and hopped up into Tinker's jacket sleeve. Mind you, looking back, the line-up seemed more relieved that those nuisances had been seen off, some even waved. Hey, another public service by your friendly neighbourhood biker.

Fifteen minutes later his small glow of duty done was abruptly snuffed by familiar patriotic-coloured flashers and the commanding whoop of a police siren. A white BMW bike had snuck up on him; you'd think the fuzz would at least have the decency to buy British.

"Play dead," Tinker whispered to Bonzo. The pup had peeked out of his jacket, and gorphons have this instinctual thing about uniforms—as his long-suffering postie recently found out.

The officer lifted up the visor on his full-face; strutted over, taking his time. Young, cocky, Tinker had his measure from the get go.

"Hmm," the bike fuzz walked slowly around Poke, curling his lip. "Old Indian, huh? Maybe if they'd made a proper motorcycle like mine their factory would still be in business."

Tinker smiled affably. "They did. Model 841 WWII desert issue: transverse 750cc V-twin, unit construction, foot shift, shaft drive, hydraulically damped front end and spring-heel rear. Impressed the Italian troops so much they immediately ran away home to copy them for Moto-Guzzi." He looked pointedly at the police bike. "Thought the BMW boys lost the war."

Policemen don't much care to be corrected, and his tone chilled into formality. "Were you playing guitar at the Odeon cinema queue, sir?"

The bloody great twelve-string case on Tinker's back constituted a fair cop. "Yeah, I were busking," he admitted. "What's the big deal?"

Ignoring him, the cop regarded Poke's leather saddlebags with suspicion. "You wouldn't by any chance have a small dog in there?"

Tinker gave him the kind of look you reserve for defectives, sighed, and dismounted. He slipped off the guitar case, opening it to confirm only the Stella was in residence. Next he unbuckled the bags and pulled out the contents: raingear, tool roll, can of tyre inflator, small fire extinguisher etc.—biker's equivalent of a large lady's handbag, and not so much as a doggie biscuit in sight. He held open his leather jacket and theatrically unzipped the cuffs. "Observe, boys and girls, nothing up my sleeves."

Sarcasm apparently didn't tickle the fuzz's fancy. "Several young men have complained of having a vicious dog set on them by a biker. They said he'd been annoying the queue with persistent begging and obnoxious songs."

On reflection, perhaps Tinker could have cut some of the Billy Connolly-inspired patter filling in between songs and quick retunings, twelve-stringers can be absolute bastards.

'I don't have to do this for a living you know, I could be sitting on my arse at home collecting welfare' or 'You think this is shite? Wait till you see the movie' might have caused offence.

"Any complaints from my audience?" Tinker did have his performer's pride after all.

The bike cop scowled. "Actually they said it was the best show they'd seen in years . . . but that's beside the point."

For want of a dog, the officer had to settle for a close inspection of Tinker's documents and Poke's numbers. Her numbers were good, Tinker had stamped them himself, and he could pass off used arse-wipe as proper paperwork to any plod.

Disparaging remarks regarding Poke's reversion open duals led to a demand that she be fired up for a sound check. Inconspicuously turning the Edison-Splitdorf magneto to full retard, Tinker complied. Poke chuffed away slow and sleepy; too quiet for the officer who reached over and opened the throttle wide. Needless to say, the motor wouldn't rev and bogged when he tried snapping the twist grip.

"Sicc'em, Bonzo," whispered Tinker. When he'd leaned over to retard the mag, the tiny gorphon had crawled from his sleeve and down to the ground. You can get real close to your gorphon, sense each others' thought processes, know what each must do. That's how man came to hunt with dogs and ride on horses—symbiosis, old magics are always the best.

The policeman returned the papers with an ill-grace. The hard stare he gave Tinker didn't encompass a scurrying little brindled beastie.

"On yer bike," he groused. "I see you with that dog, it's getting destroyed. Mind now, I'll be watching your arse."

Stuffing the docs away, Tinker fumbled and one fell on Poke's far side. While reaching down to pick it up, he advanced the mag and Bonzo crawled quickly back up his sleeve.

"Better you should watch your own," said Tinker, clearing Poke's carbon with serious postern blasts. He popped the foot clutch, breaking loose his rear rubber, and tore away.

Cursing, the cop hit the starter, dumped the clutch, and broke loose his tyre too—right off the rim. Poke's throaty idle had covered the hiss of escaping air as tiny adamantine teeth masticated the beemer's sidewall. Generally not recommended to attempt drag racing on a completely flat tyre,

Looking back, Tinker and Bonzo watched the fuzz lose control as the torn rubber carcass locked up the wheel, stuffing his bike into a parked car. Now there was a sight as called for a drink.

Poke sat parked up behind the pub at the beer garden gate. Tinker tossed back his dram of single malt, chasing it with a swill of ale. He filled the whisky glass with beer and set it down as a well-earned reward for little Bonzo. There being no other customers around to object, he got out the Stella. After a moment's thought, he remembered Long John Baldry's song about his own run-in with the Law while busking. On the stand the musically-challenged plod had accused Baldry of playing the naughty 'boodgie-woodgie'. How did that chorus go?

"So don't try to lay no boodgie woodgie on the King of Rock and Roll,"

ALFIE

Tinker had felt it coming, already in his leathers when the phone rang. He really didn't want to answer it.

"Yeah . . . That's me . . . Which hospital . . . I'm on my way."

Tinker sucked in his breath between clenched teeth and punched the wall.

"Ah shit," he groaned. "Not Alfie."

Christ! He realised he'd just blown through another stop sign. There wasn't any time to lose, however Tinker figured he'd arrive faster on Poke than in the back of an ambulance, and slowed down.

Alfie, why did it have to be Alfie? He'd been like the father Tinker never had. A man's man and a dyed-in-the-leathers Harley rider; unfortunately no one rides forever, not that hard.

People got out of the big biker's way as he strode intently down the corridor. Tinker tried to avoid hospitals and cemeteries; too much pain, too many voices. As a gypsy cursed with second sight he'd learned to tune out soul-static. It had been either that or go doolally. Right now his psychic senses were straining for a particular voice, and it seemed very faint.

Alfie lay propped up in bed with more tubes and sensor lines than an Italian wiring harness. His long white hair lay brushed out in neat waves on the pillow and he was unconscious. Tinker looked down into that familiar, well-mapped face; without Alfie's animating spirit it was an old man's. Each battle scar had its story and Tinker had heard them all—this body had been lived in.

An eye opened, and Alfie grinned behind his oxygen mask. "Battery died, Tink" he whispered. "I didn't take the hint, so now it's my turn."

No, you tried to bump-start the Evo, Tinker realised. Alfie had traded in his beloved Hydra Glide for a lard-arsed Soft Tail look-alike when the cardiologist forbade any further kick starting. Of course it would have to have been the bike, or a punch-up, or women. Alfie had treated the mounting years like miles per hour and just kept going faster. Sure didn't look like he'd be making the ton today.

Alfie's big-knuckled hand found Tinker's and gave a weak squeeze. He used to crush beer cans between finger and thumb to hear them swoosh. "Tinker," he said, pulling off the mask. "You know that magic shite you're into, the stuff we don't ever talk about?"

Tinker coloured beneath his black beard. Alfie didn't miss much. "I never wanted you mixed up in that," he muttered. "Magic is worse than crack cocaine; it makes you offers you can't refuse."

"Refusal ain't exactly an option here either," Alfie observed dryly. "That's why I asked 'em to call you—I could use a bit of that magic, like."

Tinker's face fell. "Alfie," he said, as gently as he could. "I can't work miracles."

"I should hope not," snapped an anorexic young nurse, bustling in with her clipboard. Florence Nightingale definitely wouldn't have approved of the abbreviated Victorian uniform; for one thing, the material was mourning-black bombazine. She checked Alfie's pulse against the upside-down watch pinned on her washboard-flat chest, then glared at Tinker. "Rather late for visitors, isn't it?"

Alfie stared at her suspiciously. "Hoi, I've not seen you before, what's yer game?"

Tinker had, although most mortals only got to see her once, and as for the game . . . He squeezed Alfie's hand tight. "It's her, Alfie, The one I can't stop. Nobody can stop Death."

Alfred Fitzherbert Smith nodded, and set a big-boned jaw. "Help me up on my pillows, Tink," he said, "and offer the lady a seat." He looked up at Death. "Better to see eye to eye, like."

"I always come in person for the brave ones," she confided to Tinker as he got her a chair. "Bangs are more fun than whimpers."

Alfie wheezed with laughter and reached under his pillow, pulling out a forbidden pack of fags. Tinker looked around for smoke detectors and the oxygen tank valve. Then he noticed the watch on Death's black pinafore, the second hand had stopped. She can do that with time; few entities can.

Death smiled, showing small white teeth. "Always time for a last cigarette, Alfie, but you're not condemned . . . yet."

Alfie's granite grey eyes looked into hers with a twinkle of mica. "Any chance of a bevvie then?"

"Not doctor approved," said a new voice. A man dressed as a surgeon stood in the doorway. He looked like he'd just come from some hideously botched operation. The face was hidden by the mask, but of course he wasn't a man. He gestured disdainfully at Tinker with a bloody glove. "Is this the sinner's advocate, a gutter-wizard? I'll be back at the torture block in no time."

A touch of colour tinged Death's wan cheeks. "Demon," she enunciated coldly. "We cannot hear you. You are improperly gowned."

The demon bowed in apology, then tossed his gloves and stained surgical greens into a corner, revealing formal court attire. Clawed hands swept off the cap and wavy white hair flowed to his shoulders like an advocates wig. Alfie gasped as the blotched surgical mask slipped off. It was like looking into a mirror—at a carnival.

Tinker swallowed. That face could be exhibit A. The same water buffalo forehead, flattened nose, thick sensual lips and a jaw like a pit bull. At best it was never the face of innocence, but the demon's version of Alfie was more like the picture of Dorian Gray.

"Objection," said Tinker, careful to stand first. You don't address the beak sitting on your butt. "Characterisation, highly prejudicial."

Death considered. "No, I'll allow it. He has to put the worst face on things."

Yeah, Edward bleedin' Hyde, thought Tinker, bowing to her decision.

The evil Alfie smirked. "I regret to observe that my learned friend is not gowned either.'

Tinker had thought of that. "Apologies, my lady, I was not notified of trial until this moment. However I shall conduct myself sky-clad, should the court so desire."

Death smiled thinly. She liked impudent rogues and naked was the formal dress of magic. "Tempting, but unnecessary. We recognise lay advocates."

"That's a relief," grunted Alfie, and gave Tinker an encouraging wink.

The demon rose like a pantomime devil and extended his robe theatrically. His arm fell, and a young boy in an out-of-date school uniform stood revealed. He dripped dirty water and was long dead.

"Blurry 'ell," gasped Alfie. "Andy the Pansy."

"Tell the nice people, young Andrew," coaxed the demon.

"B . . . big bully," stuttered the boy, pointing a water-wrinkled finger at Alfie. "He had them all p . . . picking on me. It got so I just c . . . couldn't stand it any longer."

Tinker leaned towards his client and whispered urgently in his ear. "I'm gonna have to put you under the 'fluence. You'll have to trust me on this." With pinky and forefinger, Tinker drew down Alfie's eyelids. The breathing grew shallow.

"I call young Alfie for rebuttal," Tinker announced. "Audio only, under the circumstances."

A child's voice issued from Alfie's lips, uncoarsened by drink and tobacco. "Caught him trying on his sister's clothes, didn't I. Too stuck-up to play with us, always hanging around the girls—he's just a great, big sissy."

"I hate you," Andrew burst out, losing his stutter in pure rage. "I'd do anything to see you burn in Hell like me."

"Order!" said Death sharply, and Andrew was gone, taking his puddle with him.

"I . . . it was me found him in the canal," continued young Alfie, a quaver in his voice. "I dived in and got him, tried to pump the water out but it was too late. Papers said I was a little hero—me as did it surely as if I'd p . . . pushed him in."

Tinker hurriedly snapped his fingers before Alfie talked himself deeper into it.

"Hoi, wot's all this then?" Alfie demanded, brushing away childhood tears.

"Just kid's stuff," said his demon doppelganger, smiling nastily. "Let's see what's on the telly." He swung the set around so they all could see it. "Hmm, channel '51 I think."

It was a black and white BBC newscast. "Chinese launch offensive . . . American forces in full retreat . . . Our boys cut off . . ."

Tinker knew all about Korea. Every anniversary Alfie told the same story improved by ale and the years. "The bloody ROK bugged-out again and then the Yanks buggered off . . ." he'd begin.

Alfie's eyes were glued to footage of advancing quilt-jacketed hordes, but his lips moved. "Began with the bugles, then they'd charge. First wave had grenades, second had rifles, third had fuck-all but what they could pick as they followed. Thank Christ we had the water-cooled Vickers, the lads were pissing on red-hot Brens and mortars—pissing our pants too."

The demon turned from the screen. "You were professional British soldiers well dug-in on a hill with organised fields of fire, large quantities of ammunition, plus full air and long range artillery support." He pointed a claw at the close-up of a wounded Chinese soldier lying amongst a field of corpses. "This newly conscripted peasant had neither training nor transport, only what he stood up in and five days worth of cooked rice. There was neither support nor supply; he scavenged from his own dead to survive."

Death nodded. "I recall it was a busy day." Her polished black nails drummed on the chair arm. "Your point?"

The demon twin turned to Alfie. "How many of these unfortunates did you kill?"

Alfie seemed nervous. "I dunno, can't even remember how many ammo belts I pumped through the Vickers. Couldn't see the ground for their dead."

The demon regarded its claws. "But not all were dead, hmm?"

Alfie's face hardened till it wasn't far off the demon's. "Some would fake it all day just to creep up at night with their potato mashers. I took care of that."

"I think finishing off the enemy wounded is a more candid description," observed the demon. The soldier on the screen was suddenly pinned to the ground by a bayonet.

Alfie's face remained set. "No one was taking any prisoners. Only fifty of us got out alive."

Tinker groaned. "It was war," he pleaded. "Alfie was just a teenager strung-out on too much adrenalin and too little sleep. It's a wonder he didn't go berserk."

The demon did horrible stretchy things to the face he was wearing. "Oh, you mean like a Celtic warrior's warp-spasm? Just a temporary insanity. Better now thanks, can I go home?" He attempted an expression of hand-wringing innocence with Alfie's borrowed face; it was even worse than the spasm. "Next you'll claim demoniacal possession and be blaming the prosecution."

The real Alfie growled. "Me head was on straight and it don't spin around. Maybe those choggies were just poor scared buggers like us, kids' pictures in their wallets 'n all. You've no time to think about that when thousands of the little yellow fuckers are screaming up the hill at yer."

Tinker gave it another try. "The point is, surely, that neither side had any control over their fate. They had only one law to obey, the oldest imperative—survival, kill or be killed."

Death nodded. "Even the gods must bow to necessity," she quoted.

The demon cut off the TV with an impatient gesture. "So, the insensitive bully, the desperate teen." He turned to Alfie and snarled, showing more teeth than human. "But what, Mr. Big, what pathetic excuse will the man invent to squirm off a hook?"

Tinker had to hold Alfie down. It scared him how little effort it took.

"If I were the man I was," growled Alfie, "I'd kick in yer pathetic excuse for knackers."

The demon's face assumed a lascivious expression. "Ah yes, such trouble the gonads give poor mortals. Hmm? However, since you open that door . . ."

Tinker looked sharply at Alfie, who looked down regretfully at his crotch. So it wasn't going to be Queensbury rules now, and Alfie a terror with the ladies from day one.

"But that's how us humans get here," Tinker said. "We were created to be fruitful and multiply."

The demon shrugged off the scriptures. "But not every fruit, certainly not the green ones . . ." he paused and let his mask of Alfie undergo the degenerative effects of several generations of inbreeding, " . . . and never, ever, from your own tree."

This time Tinker really did have to strain holding Alfie down; IVs and pick-ups tore off, but the monitors remained frozen in time. Tinker grabbed the fags, lit one, and stuffed it in Alfie's mouth. "As counsel I suggest you shut your fucking gob," he hissed. "We could be in trouble here."

Alfie subsided, but his face was a mirror to the demon's—guilty as sin.

"This is merely speculative. Alfie never married, never had any known offspring," Tinker said, with more assurance than he felt.

"With your permission," said the demon silkily. "Witness for the prosecution." He made a deep bow to Death. When the demon straightened up again, he was a she.

A tall girl; young, pale, big grey eyes, long blond hair streaming down the black silk court gown she clutched about her. Tinker just knew she'd have nothing on underneath. She looked a little drunk, a little scared and, Tinker hated to admit it, a little like Alfie. The miniature version of that iron jaw tightened.

"I was fifteen," she said. "He was all in leather and had a big shiny bike like in the pictures. No one knew him at the party but nobody dared say anything. He was a lot older and a whole lot tougher." Her heavy lower lip wobbled. "My mum was too messed up to care what time I got in, and who knew who my real dad was. I knew I didn't have no future, so I intended to have now."

She managed a wan smile. "We'd both been drinking scrumpy and he had some really good dope. Up close, as his zippo lit the spliff, I could see he was much older than me, but so—I dunno—in command of the grown-up world I wanted."

Unconsciously she raised a hand to her hair. "It was a warm night and the ride real exciting, his laugh so confident as he ground sparks off the footboards in the corners just to hear me squeal. We parked right on the beach. The moon was all full of cider and romance; tide was up so we went skinny-dipping.

"The sea must have been freezing, but I didn't really notice. I did notice it wasn't shrinking him any, he seemed hard all over. He was a grown man too, not like those 'Boy Georges' back at their feeble party."

Tinker risked a glance at Alfie. The tears were rolling down lined cheeks and his big hands were trembling.

"But this is mere titillation," Tinker objected desperately.

"It is not titillating me," said Death coldly. "Pray continue."

The girl shot a look at Alfie. The expression was hard to read, her face couldn't keep still.

"I . . . I pretended I had a cramp," she began hesitantly. "He carried me ashore like I was a feather in his arms. I never felt so safe, so happy."

Alfie forced himself up. "Guilty as charged," he rasped. "She don't have to say no more."

"It's not that easy," Tinker whispered, pushing him back down. "This is just a foretaste of Hell."

The girl pulled the robe tighter, the words had to come. "He smelled of salt and tobacco, hot oil and apples. When we kissed it was like a missing piece of me fell into place."

Tinker felt Alfie wince beneath his restraining hands.

"I was a virgin, then I wasn't. It hurt, but it hurt more to stop. Everything so perfect, and everything all wrong."

"Still, Alfie wasn't actually culpable," interjected Tinker. "It's not like either of them knew."

Alfie's voice came very quiet. "Her mum had been a right looker too. It was like turning back the clock over fifteen years seeing this girl at the party."

Tinker ran shaky fingers through his long black curls. "Christ, Alfie," he hissed in a cauliflowered ear, "tell me you didn't know she was yer own daughter."

Alfie let out a great sigh. "No, I didn't—not then anyhow." His fingers scrabbled on the bedclothes like a man in quicksand. "I was feeling no pain and this young bint were burning a hole in the back of my leathers."

Tinker sneaked a look at Death. It didn't look good.

"But shagging on the beach and getting into the Pope stroke, I was starin' at the moon in her eyes. Suddenly I saw myself looking back—then I knew," Alfie confessed.

"We both did," said the girl. "It didn't stop us though. We never spoke on the ride back and I never saw him again."

There was nothing to say. In the silence, Tinker heard something. A dripping tap—not a tap. The girl was standing in a slow spreading pool of blood.

"I . . . I couldn't let it live . . . couldn't afford a proper, you know . . . something went wrong."

Tinker could guess the rest. Poor bitch didn't get much fun after all, and there's none for sinners in Hell.

A swirl of black robes and the demon resumed Alfie's form. It spread its claws wide, flexed, and folded them. "I rest my case."

Tinker thought furiously of the old Perry Mason manoeuvres, Daniel Webster appeals, and all of Magic John's hard-earned training.

Then he looked at Alfie, and Alfie looked back. Alfie who'd taught him how to ride, but despaired of ever teaching him how to fight dirty. The Alfie who'd fix your bike but steal your girlfriend. And finally an Alfie who'd met all his ghosts and just needed a last kind word, the defence's summation. Tinker got to his feet.

"Alfie here was, and remains, my hero. Maybe I've had the rare chance to see my idol's feet of clay, but it's only made him more of a real man. Alfie was far too alive to be all good; he offers no excuses and has never begged for mercy."

Tinker laid a hand on broad, boney shoulders. "He's completely guilty of being human and being human, we suffer, we sin and we die. The little pansy, the party girl, that poor bloody coolie even, they should never have become playthings for a demon. The entire human race can look forward to hell if such harsh judgements are going to prevail."

The demon grinned hugely at the prospect, yet Death frowned.

"Born, sin, die, go straight to hell—done deal. Not much of a game that," Tinker said resignedly. "Bit predictable and boring, when you think about it."

Now the demon started developing a scowl.

"Thing I wonder about," mused Tinker out loud. "How are all those guardian angels going to take being made redundant? Nothing on their lily-white hands but eternity and mischief. Frankly, I could see a re-harrowing of Hell."

The demon was sweating now; certainly Alfie's face had never looked that scared. It directed a mute appeal to Death, who considered, then extended a fist with the thumb out horizontal—slowly she raised a black-nailed forefinger in the air. The letter of judgement.

The demon forced out a nod like his neck was being broken, then went looking for things to smash.

Tinker whirled and grabbed Alfie out of the bed. Ignoring popping lines and tubes, he danced him around the room laughing.

"L for Life, Alfie, Life. We won, you got Li . . ." Tinker's voice died away. Alfie hung so light and limp in his arms.

A cold hand touched Tinker's shoulder.

"My partner, I think," Death said, slipping herself between him and Alfie. "L is for Limbo *sine die* or perhaps in your case, for learner's luck."

The demon held the door open as she waltzed a *dance macabre* around the room. "But you are right, Tinker," she whispered over Alfie's shoulder. "It would be far too boring."

Death switched to a polka and whisked him out.

The demon hopped from one hoof to the other in the doorway. He looked uncomfortable, embarrassed.

Tinker sat down on the edge of the bed and waved him away. "Yeah, yeah, I won't tell, but now you owe me your name." He picked up a white pillow feather from the floor then regarded the ceiling nervously. "Oh dear, now you don't suppose . . ." The demon disappeared in a puff of sulphur.

Tinker had to stop a couple of times on the road home and wipe his goggles. They kept fogging up inside.

Limbo, sine die, he thought, for the umpteenth time. Not exactly the Elysian Fields or Valhalla, but at least it wasn't Hell and somehow he couldn't see Alfie in Heaven.

"Oh, Alfie," Tinker whispered into the wind.

TIME PASSAGES

First a couple of spots on his Paulson bubble goggles, then down it came like the judgment of God. Tinker was too close to home for rain-suit wrestling and too far to outrun this deluge. The back road followed an old railway embankment; with any luck . . . There, a small side street cut under the line; a dirty brick-lined tunnel, passage really, barely wide enough for one car.

Raining like the proverbial diabetic cow pissing on a flat rock, thought Tinker. Cutting the big Vee, he removed his vintage half-helmet, and dismounted. Tinker was struck with the memory of how he used to duck into these tunnels as a kid just to feel the trains hammer overhead, shaking the very ground. He could recall vividly the anticipation as one drew nearer in a mounting crescendo of steam-driven iron. Good timing, here came one now.

The years evaporated as Tinker crouched down, holding his breath. Over and over ran the great steel wheels, then away with a rush, and a rattle, and a roar. He ran out the other end in time to see the guard's van receding wreathed in smoke, cursing as he caught a hot cinder in the eye. He managed to blink it out, looked around, and then stopped. It wasn't raining; in fact, this street looked bone dry. He walked back to the Vee's end. Still tossing cats and dogs, hmmm! Turning up his collar, Tinker ventured into the rain to check.

No sign of any train, hardly surprising as the tracks were torn up some thirty years ago. Tinker shook rain from his ample black beard as he stumped back to the far end. Sunshine glistened on polished iron converging to infinity. Definitely not Kansas, Toto.

A car puttered past, a Ford Popular, Tinker hadn't seen one since he was a lad. A boy running along the opposite pavement stopped, gawping at this wet, leathered-clad apparition. Wearing some kind of private school uniform: gray flannel shorts, tie, school cap even. A woman caught up with him, stalled in a momentary stare at Tinker, then prodded her offspring along smartish. She wore the most unlikely hat with half a bird pinned to it and, watching her hasty retreat, seams in the back of her nylon stockings.

Some riders would shrug, weather can be weird and people weirder. Others might think to lay off the funny pills. Most wouldn't know what to think. Tinker, however, being something of a gutter-mage on wheels, got it first time.

"What you got here, my wee man," Tinker muttered to himself, "is a time tunnel."

Tinker fired up Pocahontas, his Indian Scout bar-hopper, and performed a mental check as she warmed her fifty-weight oil. Old fivers from a coin collector, wind-up watch, nothing with a date or high-tech. He'd been doing his homework; time tunnels, apart from being rare as Amish hotrods, were activated by strong emotions, vivid memories. With sufficient concentration you could dial up a specific date in your life. However they only worked in time, not space, so he needed period wheels and that ruled out the Super Vee. Poke's first screams rattled the Wigwam racing department windows in nineteen forty-eight, about the time baby Tinker was doing the same in a small Scottish but 'n ben.

Ready as he'd ever be; time to hit the road.

Keeping Poke grumbling in second gear, Tinker held to the speed limit; noticeably less traffic in the early sixties. First stop was the nearest bookie in time for closing bets. He'd been checking race results in his local library microfiche and selected a few high-odds winners.

Finances having been secured, it was off to Claude Ryan's bike parts emporium to loot their war surplus Indian mother lode. Bulging saddlebags later, he was purchasing a post office box and a money order to 'Exchange & Mart'. An ad for Indian magnetos, speedometers, transmission gears and, optimistically, performance parts to be placed in the next few editions.

His stomach grumbled for lunch, so Tinker took Poke out west on the North Circular to stretch her ever-willing legs. He misted up seeing the old Ace Café at Stonebridge Park with a couple of serious ton-up bikes parked amongst the wannabe Tiger Cubs and Bantams.

Poke was given dismissive looks as Tinker putted into the lot. These rockers had only known the de-tuned military Junior Scouts: run forever, sixty never. After Tinker burned a feet-on-pegs hot rubber doughnut, they both received the respect due their years. Rounds of condensed-milk enriched tea, sausage sarnies, and a carton of fags passed out soon had Tinker's engineer boots well under the formica-topped table.

Everybody had a dad or uncle who'd owned an Indian. *Grandfathers in my time*, Tinker realized. Sure, they'd see if any parts were still in the shed, ask around. Be something in it for them.

Weeks passed, Tinker's garage grew chocker with highly desirable items fabricated entirely from unobtanium and costing him sweet fanny adams, courtesy of those infallible gee-gees. Yet rare parts, money even, they're all just things really once you got plenty.

Inevitably, happily, Tinker felt himself surrendering to the siren song of his zeitgeist, and it never sang sweeter than mid-sixties to seventies. An older, Norvin-riding rocker told him about the Gene Vincent gig—the leather limper's very last tour, Tinker recalled. Soon he was picking all the best tunes: Steeleye Span at Hammersmith Odeon tossing their entire night's take, some eight thousand pounds, over the audience. Captain Beefheart in his trailer at Knebworth sharing beat poetry and an after-show bottle of Drambuie. Arsing around the West End in a spiffy S.S. uniform with Moon the Loon and Bonzo Dog's Viv Stanshall. Such splendid naughties, you just had to be there.

Right place, right time—every time.

Riding back with due care and attention from an early Stones gig on Eel Pie Island, Tinker noted a distinct absence of pain. He'd followed the darkened river and taken back roads to the tunnel through a gentle haze of Moroccan hash and Newky Broon loony-soup. Fortunately Poke was a 'guid cuddie', a faithful iron pony who'd see her master home drunk or deranged, especially if she wanted that winter rebuild.

Tinker listened as Poke's full-retard chuffing echoed inside the tunnel, then he grounded the magneto. It always took a few moments concentration to summon future-present; more than a few lately. He frowned, banishing the hash-jinns and miner's ruin from his brain. Now! A car cruised past the far end, typical late model import, yet it somehow didn't seem as . . . well, as real as the past.

Tinker swivelled around in the saddle and looked back. Even the stars there seemed brighter; cleaner air, less photo-contamination. He could reach out and catch them now. Yeah, all his favourite stars, even the dead ones, and on their best nights too. Reliving those incandescent moments again and again—how do you resist that?

Riding home, Tinker's frown deepened, and it wasn't at the late-night drunks swerving all over the road in their nasty little modern cars.

"What you got here, pilgrim," he grunted, "is a temptation."

For the next week or so, Tinker concentrated on a long-overdue top 'n bottoming of the house, even weeding the neglected garden. He got out more and renewed auld acquaintances: couple of sealed fifty tins of Capstan Full-Strength for Red the Ted, a dozen Bass No. 1 ales for Magic John, a few choice period custom parts for riding pals. Everyone wanted more, so did Tinker. Same answer; won't be going there again.

It hurt like giving up a drug, or a lover, and of course everything reminded Tinker of those good old days. Sure didn't help his place being crammed with fifties Eagle and sixties underground comics, shellac blues records, yellowing photo albums.

Tinker caught himself with an open photo album before him on the kitchen table, a hash-spiked joint smouldering unheeded in the deco glass ashtray.

Windows, he'd been looking through windows into his past. Thing being, now he could do more than look, lots more.

The album shut with a bang—this was lap dancing for the heart. He could still see the snapshot's after-image, a young couple on an early chop. He knew exactly where and when. Hadn't he tortured himself over every nuance of that moment?

It was Jean, of course: the one, the first, the only true love of his bachelor life. A younger, skinnier Tinker held her tight. Alas, not tight enough.

He could be in that picture, off somewhere in the fuzzy background, watching out for them, like. Only watching, he told himself, just watching and waiting for the past to catch up.

She'd be dead within six months, only his unborn son was meant for the chop. Junkie back-street abortionist hadn't meant to die either. Careless mistakes come with a price, like ground glass for lunch. Tinker had never even known she was pregnant till the autopsy. Suddenly he realized that he didn't have that excuse any more. Now he had the choice; pre-choice actually. Nobody had to die.

Caught in a blitzkrieg of temptation, you either surrender immediately or fight to the death.

A tall shadow picked its way between darkened tents and slumbering bikes. Across a wooded field the young man could see the cheerful lights of the beer tent beckoning and it sounded like the band was warming up in the marquee. Jean would be there with her girlfriends, still laughing because he'd forgotten to chain up the bike.

The moon slipped demurely from her cloud petticoats, and the shadow froze.

"Man!" Tinker whistled. "What a cool Indian." A Comanche war-pony to his Harley plough-horse, it looked fast just sitting there under a tree. "Someday," he vowed softly, and knew he would make it come true.

Suddenly he became aware of eyes at his back. Tinker was learning to trust his extra gypsy senses and could feel: inspection, anxiety, possessiveness. He turned quickly and caught a big bloke observing him from the shadows of a large tent. The man didn't move, yet Tinker picked up a surge of strong emotions.

"Just looking," Tinker hastily assured. There was an aura of danger around both the bike and its mysterious owner. "I've a Harley 45 bobber."

"Red metal-flake tanks, silver frame, '43 WLC, clutch throw-out bearing near shot." The stranger's voice came muffled through the scarf over his lower face, eyes unreadable behind shades. "I've been looking too." He stepped out of the shadows and moonlight puddled on black leathers, caught silver threads in a long mane of wind-tousled jet hair.

Tinker didn't feel entirely sure he appreciated that much attention. However there was something compelling about this old biker that held him from the pleasures awaiting. All this apparition needed was a dead albatross round his neck.

"I . . . was really looking at Jean." The burly rider blurted it out like a confession. He flinched, and not from Tinker's reaction. Where Jean was concerned, neither size nor numbers mattered: instinctively, Tinker had adopted a fighting stance.

"That's the girl I'm going to marry," he warned.

"Pity you've not told her that," mumbled the stranger into his scarf. "I'm an old . . . friend of Jean's," he said, coming closer. "Kinda unofficial guardian angel, like. Just call me Arch."

Tinker felt a common chord, his mother had insisted on Archibald. Being part-gypsy, the school bullies' taunt had been 'dirty tinky'. He'd adopted it as a badge of pride; besides, anything was better than Archibald.

He relaxed and held out an open hand. "Any friend of Jean's is a friend of mine. Tinker's the name."

Arch kept his hands behind his back. "No offense . . . ah, Tinker. Any contact is a risk. Hell, I shouldn't even be talking to you."

Now the guy looked too husky to have leprosy; still, he sure seemed worried about something. Tinker, however, could look deeper than most and wanted to get to the bottom of this. He focused the second-sight that had come intertwined with his father's gypsy genes. *Okay chum,* he thought, *let's cop a quick gander at you.*

Tinker stiffened. The 'sight revealed a tattooed Pict warrior leaning on a great stone-headed axe, laughing and pointing. The figure shifted and before him stood an arch-wizard with white hair and beard to the waist. The air crackled about the mage as he frowned, and the deep-sunk eyes burned with a green fire. They were set in the same, oddly familiar face.

The vision fell apart as Tinker blinked in astonishment, leaving him staring at the big biker before him. Arch had to be that same man, if man he was at all, and not the least bit happy.

"Dammit, I shoulda remembered the 'sight," Arch grumbled, then collected himself with a shake. "This can't be happening. I'm so outta here."

Tinker became acutely conscious that he stood between Arch and his bike. Also, but for that odd aversion to physical contact, Arch could plough right through him. Nevertheless, he held out a warding hand.

"Hang on a bit," he said resolutely. "There's more to this than you're saying. For starters, you're not from around here, not with those tyres."

Arch smote himself on the forehead. "Only the best skins for Poke," he muttered bitterly. Even the compounds in those racing radials hadn't been invented yet. He sighed, took off his shades and pulled the scarf from his face. "Okay, our kid. Now we do it the hard way."

Tinker hadn't been listening; he was reflecting—emerald eye to emerald eye.

"Dad?" he gasped uncertainly. Sean O'Toole split when his son started school, only the fading memory since.

To his surprise the biker burst out laughing. "No, little Tinker, the child is the father of the man." The laughter died. "Sean is of the past. I'm the future—yours actually."

Tinker's eyes bugged out. He knew truth when it bit him in the balls. "You mean . . . you're me? From the future?"

Arch wouldn't meet his eyes. He was muttering to himself like a loonie " . . . of course . . . never realised . . . all along, it was me." He nodded reluctantly, sighed, and seemed to brace himself for the inevitable.

"Far out! And that's your time machine?" Young Tinker turned to stare at the Scout. Made it half-way, then the lights went out.

Tinker dropped the thick branch he'd been holding and looked around casually. No witnesses. Hefting his younger self over to the shadows of the big tent, he rifled his jacket and pocketed the wallet. Old Tinker sighed and kissed a bloody forehead; he pushed Poke to the exit before firing her up.

Riding after dark is always a time for remembering the past, and it was tense tonight. Fortunately, apart from working the ponies, an advantage of full retrospection is you can ensure synchronicity even while playing an active part.

He still had the scar under his wind-blown hair, still free to fly without helmet laws for a couple of years yet. Hit from behind at that old, yet unforgettable, rally he'd only just left. Jean would prove very sympathetic tonight and they'd get drunk on her money, too drunk to care for the morrow or remember any precautions. It had been the best night of his young life.

Tinker had always wanted to meet up with the bastard who'd mugged him, he'd picked up the stick there just in case. Unfortunately he could never recall a damn thing about who did him. Now he knew why.

He also knew he could go back and save Jean, then fast-forward home to her waiting arms and a fine, grown-up son. All it would cost was his life's work—himself. Altering the time continuum doesn't come cheap—it's life for life. There couldn't be room for two futures, only one, and this Tinker wouldn't be in it.

On the other side of the tunnel, Tinker took out the stolen wallet and extracted the photo of Jean, the only copy he would ever have. So young then, striking rather than merely beautiful, a face fated never to be fine-tuned by character and a life lived. Had Jean been born a man, she'd still have been his best pal. It was her spirit, her soul, Tinker loved; and like the photo, it lay in his hands. He could have the memory, but not the reality, at least not him.

That was toll for the tunnel and when it came to the nut, he couldn't cut it. Tears of betrayal stung his eyes. Turning in the saddle Tinker looked back at the tunnel's mouth; a hungry hole in the arm, a scab you could never stop guiltily picking.

"What you got here, sucker," he hissed through clenched teeth as he banged Poke into first, "is a trap."

Wind sighed through the tunnel. It didn't like to lose. It did, however, possess great patience. After all, it had all the time in the world.

Printed in the United States
137901LV00008B/105/P